THE
MOONGLOW CAFE

A Paige MacKenzie Mystery

Deborah Garner

Cranberry Cove Press

The Moonglow Café
by Deborah Garner

First Printing – April 2014
ISBN: 978-0-9960449-1-2

Printed in the U.S.A.

Also by Deborah Garner

Above the Bridge

To Bear

PROLOGUE

Jonas slid his hands along the cold, clammy surface. In the darkness, he could only *feel* the uneven lumps of clay, could only use his fingers to search, not his eyes. Day after day, week after week, year after year it had been like this. Every spring he began, hopeful, and every summer he remained determined. But now the sinking feeling that always accompanied late autumn had settled in. As the temperatures fell outside, so did his spirits. Another year gone, fruitless.

Stay focused. What was it you were looking for?

He had known once, long ago, back when everything made sense, before the clouds began to form, and the strokes of blue faded. Now he searched aimlessly. Momentum pulled him without direction. He was its slave.

Some days he thought he saw blurred images beyond the sky – tiny wisps of color or the strands of a horse's mane, sienna splashes, a feathered headdress. Or was it a cottonwood tree? His eyes deceived him. His mind deceived him.

It is pitch black, but should be gold as rolling hills, blue as sapphires. Where were the colors, where was the light?

He lifted his hands from the surface and cradled his face. The smell of dirt filled his nostrils, and cool grit scratched his skin. Wrinkles against wrinkles; time had lost its meaning. Where had the years gone?

He let his arms drop, took a step back, and the chill enfolded him. It was always this way, airy, yet impenetrable. The chill always won. Every match struck was soon extinguished. Sometimes he wondered why he kept trying at all.

Keep going. It is waiting for you. Don't give up.

He slapped at the cold surface, felt the ridges and specks of embedded twigs and stones. Frustrated, he balled one hand into a fist and punched the wall, hitting the sharp edge of a rock. Pain soared up his forearm.

You're a fool. You'll be searching forever. There's nothing here but your own mind's confusion.

This voice was wrong. He would not accept it, even if it would not leave him be. How could a voice, disembodied, know more than he did? So many years of waiting and wondering – wasn't effort to be rewarded?

You don't even know what you're looking for.

How he hated those words that taunted him from out of nowhere. If only his mind would be quiet, he could hear himself think. It was right in front of him or not there at all.

Raise your arm, reach on through....

Walls were his enemy, unyielding, stubborn, blinding. In darkness, they separated his soul from life. How could this shadow of himself focus? He was old. Or was he? Time felt immeasurable and meaningless. The search had been constant.

Wait! There, below your fingers....

He gasped as his hand felt an uneven lump in the dirt, but the lump smoothed back into the flat surface. It was always the same. Walls gave into no one. Defeated again, he fell to the ground and pounded it with rage.

CHAPTER ONE

Brakes squealed, and a taxi's bleating horn startled Paige back onto the curb. A burly, unshaven man leaned out the driver's window of the cab, spewed obscenities at the car in front of him and sneered at Paige as if it were her fault another driver had the decency to stop for an elderly woman crossing the busy avenue.

"Hey," Paige shouted at the taxi driver, indicating the stooped figure in front of the first car, still moving forward, one shaky tap of a cane on the asphalt at a time.

"Screw you!" the cabbie snapped back. With a sudden twist of the steering wheel, he sped around the stopped car, missing the woman by inches.

Kindness, a lost art. Patience, even more elusive. City life in all its undesirable glory.

Paige flipped up her coat's collar to fight a sudden gust of cold November wind. Holding the warm faux fur snugly around her neck, she gauged the oncoming traffic and darted between vehicles until she reached the opposite curb. The old woman had managed to make it across the street safely and was already lost in the southbound, flowing crowd. Paige checked her watch, turned north and picked up her pace. Susan was waiting.

The Manhattan Post resided on the twenty-third floor of a stately, stone and brick building that had been a New York fixture since the early 1930s when European immigrants built it. In Art Deco fashion typical of that era, intricate stonework detailed the tall, linear structure. Floral motifs and spiraling scrolls framed the rectangular windows and front entrance. Solid brass handles gripped the heavy doors.

Inside, Paige's low-heeled pumps clicked against black and white marble tiles. An elevator chime echoed across the lobby, and a flood of people surged toward the opening doors. It was full to capacity before Paige reached it, so she waited for the next one. It wouldn't matter which one she took. She always felt like one of a dozen sardines on the upward journey to the office. She tapped her foot impatiently. Eventually, she stepped into the next available elevator and endured the ride.

The return to New York after her last assignment had been stressful. The noise, congested traffic and harried pace had seemed foreign, even though she'd lived in the middle of it for years. Odd how a short time away from the city could change a person so profoundly.

As Paige passed by her editor's glass walled office, Susan waved but didn't stop pacing the floor or talking into the cell phone glued to her ear. Paige nodded a greeting in return. They'd talk over coffee later in the morning, as was their habit. Or lunch, if time allowed.

Paige's desk faced a window that looked out over the city, an advantage to having a cubicle along the side of the main room. She threw her coat over the back of her chair, sat down and rolled forward, kicking her shoes off under her desk.

Yesterday's notes, neatly clipped together, lay in one of the stacked, metal trays to her left. She'd never liked clutter and would admit readily that she was obsessively neat. A stapler, tape dispenser, pencil holder and memo pad stood directly before her. The computer screen to her right was tilted slightly at a pleasing angle. She turned on the monitor, opened her browser and brought up the morning's email.

"Anything juicy?" Even if Brandi hadn't spoken, Paige would have known it was her nosing around from the next cubicle by the waft of perfume that preceded her. The jangling of Brandi's many bracelets left no doubt. As expected, the sharp click of heels and rustling of taffeta followed the question. How Brandi picked her work outfits was something Paige found a mystery. She eyed her co-worker's magenta dress. At least the turquoise earrings and chunky, oversized rings matched each other. A purple streak in her bottle-blonde hair picked up the tone of the colorful fabric, as well.

"Not really," Paige said, scrolling down the screen and deleting spam. "How's life in Obit Land?" Brandi's answers were always entertaining.

"Some old rich lady croaked in Queens. Boring." Brandi sighed. "And a drunken teenager wrapped his new Camaro around a tree. Stupid." She flattened her hands, palms down, and spread her fingers apart. "Time for a fill." She flipped one hand upward to show Paige the space around her cuticles.

The crack of a door latch opening gave Paige an excuse to lift her eyes from feigned interest in Brandi's nails. Susan was beckoning her to her office. She closed her email and crossed the newsroom.

"Thanks for saving me," Paige said. She found Brandi adorable but distracting. Paige's regular morning meetings with Susan allowed her to get focused on work.

"Anytime," Susan replied. "Besides, I have a project that I think will interest you. In fact, it's perfect for you."

Indicating a seat for Paige to take, Susan sat down behind her desk and reached for a brochure that rested at an angle on top of a haphazard stack of papers. Susan was as messy as Paige was neat. Yet Paige knew, in a file-finding competition, Susan would be the clear winner. The system of seemingly disorganized piles of paper worked for her.

"Look at this," Susan said, handing the brochure across the desk to Paige.

When Paige glanced at the cover, her heart sank. "Symposia Gemmarum," she read quietly, noting a printed list of dates. "This is next month, here in New York City. Some kind of conference?" The brochure listed Javits Center as the location, and the 11th Avenue convention venue was well known for its massive event capacity.

"Exactly," Susan said. "A conference and exhibition for gemologists, basically. People who work with precious stones, or sell them, or process them, will come in from all over the world. This gemology organization often holds these trade shows overseas, but this year's conference is here in New York."

"Sounds interesting," Paige said, leaning back in her chair less than enthusiastically. She'd already completed two New York based articles since returning from her last out-of-state travel writing assignment. She was ready to leave town again. For the West, to be precise.

Paige thumbed through the brochure, noting dates and times. Out of habit, she started running possible angles through her mind: the international melting pot of attendees, the advanced development of gemology techniques or perhaps an evaluation of the industry within different socio-economic areas of the globe. None of these appealed to her, but she knew she could pull off whatever Susan wanted. Mustering up her professionalism, she sat up straight and waited for her editor's instructions.

"You'll need a place to stay...."

"A place to stay?" Paige asked. "I have an apartment right here in Manhattan. Well, a tiny, closet-sized space I share with three other people, but a place. It's even close to Javits Center."

"Which is exactly why it won't work for this assignment," Susan said. "I've made a list of possible accommodations for you. A few are a little off-the-beaten-path, as you like to call it. You can choose." She handed a sheet of paper to Paige, whose eyes grew wide as she scanned the assorted names.

"These are all in Montana!" Was it possible Susan was sending her back west? "What does this have to do with Symposia Gemmarum?"

Susan shuffled through some loose papers and pulled out a calendar. "It's been almost a month since we ran the Jackson Hole article. The reader response was great. Some of our subscribers wrote to tell us it was refreshing to read about another part of the country. I don't think we should wait much longer to publish the second in this series on the Old West.

"I want to run something that ties in with the gemology conference, some aspect of U.S. involvement in that industry. I think the answer lies in sapphires."

"Sapphires?" Paige repeated the word but didn't really hear what she was saying. She was still absorbing the good news that she got to go west again.

Susan laughed. "OK, Paige, snap out of it. I know you're dreaming about that favorite, sexy cowboy of yours in Wyoming, but we need to discuss business."

Paige blushed. And for good reason. The thought of seeing Jake Norris again was more than a little appealing. They'd talked regularly since she returned to New York from Jackson Hole, but seeing him in the flesh would be much more satisfying.

"You're absolutely right," Paige said apologetically. "Business it is. So, what's the tie in with Montana?" She truly was curious. Potential romance aside, the hunt for a good story always interested her. She focused her attention on what Susan was saying.

"I contacted Sid of Sid's Jewelers, and he said a good amount of sapphire mining was done in Montana. One particular mining area there produces what he described as an exceptionally fine gemstone known as the Yogo sapphire." Susan paused. "Have I hooked the research addict in you yet?"

Paige nodded.

"I don't know more than that," Susan said, "but, between the need to move on the Old West series and the timing of Symposia Gemmarum, it's a good start."

Paige was already on her feet, itching to get going. Before Susan even shooed her out the door, she was mentally tossing belongings into a suitcase, kissing New York City goodbye. And maybe kissing a certain cowboy hello.

CHAPTER TWO

Paige set her luggage down and stared at the weathered building before her. The Timberton Hotel was not at all what she had expected. Granted, it was two stories tall and had a covered porch. But where the photo on the hotel's website showed window boxes filled with daffodils, in reality only the empty boxes remained. A torn screen covered the faded gray front door, and the staggered steps that led up to it looked shaky. Paige's initial impulse was to turn around, hop into her rental car and drive the two hundred miles back to Bozeman, where her plane had landed four hours earlier.

In the end, her sense of responsibility won out, along with a smidgen of curiosity. She climbed the front steps and, after brief hesitation, pulled open the screen and knocked on the front door. It took several attempts before she got a response. When the door finally opened, a woman who was the spitting image of Aunt Bee greeted her. Reruns of *The Andy Griffith Show* instantly stood reeled and cued up in her mind.

"You must be the girl from New York," Aunt Bee said. She patted her flowery dress down against her plump waistline. "I own the hotel. My real name is Eleanor, but everyone calls me Betty." Close enough, Paige thought. Starts with a B.

As she followed the matronly hotelkeeper inside, Paige realized that the hotel's interior did not match the gloomy condition of the exterior. The neat lobby was clean and furnished with antiques. A large throw rug covered two thirds of a wooden floor, most likely original to the building. A guest registration counter stood directly across from the front entry. The square cubbyholes designed for mail that lined the back wall held keys. Carved designs decorated the woodwork below the countertop, as well as the banister of a nearby staircase that led to the second floor. The high ceiling boasted a complex pattern of tin squares. All in all, it looked welcoming. Paige's anxiety eased.

"What a lovely hotel!"

"Well, I thank you for those kind words, dear," Betty said. "It's quite a challenge to keep up with it. I've pretty much given up on the outside, but I try to keep the inside warm and cozy."

"You do a good job," Paige said. "It's very inviting, especially after a long trip." This was an understatement. She was so tired she was tempted to curl up on the lobby floor.

"So glad to hear that!" Betty was clearly pleased with the compliment. From the empty looks of the town, Paige suspected overnight guests were rare.

"Now, you go on up and choose a room. There's no one else staying here tonight, so you might as well have your pick of the litter." She waved an arm toward the staircase. "Mr. Hodges will be here tomorrow. He's a regular, comes in from Whitefish once a week for business in Anaconda. But he'll stay in number 10, down the hall here. Doesn't do stairs very well anymore, not since a bad slip on an icy patch last winter. Messed up his hip something awful." Betty shook her head and ran a sympathetic hand over her own hip. "Anyway, you go ahead and pick out any room you want. Then come on back, and we'll set you up with a registration card and key."

Burgundy floral carpeting covered the wide steps Paige climbed. The carved texture of the polished, wooden banister echoed against her skin as she skimmed one hand along it for balance. At an abrupt landing halfway up, the staircase angled sharply to the right. She followed the banister to the top.

The second floor layout was simple. One long corridor stretched from the front to the back with doors lining both sides, most propped open with brass doorstops. The rooms were similar, though not identical. All had quilts as bedcovers, whether the rooms held one full-sized bed or two twins. Other decorative touches matched each color theme. A room with a rose and cream quilt had a dark wine colored shade on a nearby table lamp. Another room, this one with twin quilts in hunter green and ivory, was graced with a rug in a dense forest pattern; creamy Aspen branches mixed with a mosaic of spring foliage.

At the end of the hallway, another sharp turn revealed a short extension with one additional room at the end. Unlike the other rooms, this one faced the rear of the property and appeared to be an addition to the original hotel building. Paige stepped inside for a closer look. Windows lined two of the walls, giving this room more light than the others. The window facing the outside of the building looked down on a side yard as barren and forlorn as the front of the hotel. The window on the opposite side showed a small patio with nothing more than a dilapidated table and one chair. Paige's guess was that the room she stood in was added above another that served as maid's quarters during busier times."

Her decision was easy. The room was light and quiet, decorated in muted shades of taupe and beige. An oval throw rug, braided with strands of dark blue and ivory, covered the floor. Ruffled shams picked up the colors of the rug, as did a variety of knick-knacks on an antique oak dresser: a perfume bottle, a crystal bud vase and a comb with a mother-of-pearl handle. The room had a spacious feel to it because of the twelve feet or so between the double bed and a writing desk against the opposite wall. Paige went downstairs to tell Betty her choice.

"Room 16, you say? All the way at the back? You sure?"

Paige laughed as she filled out the registration card. "Yes, the quiet will be good for writing and, besides, it's a nice room. Added on after the hotel was built, I'm guessing?"

Betty nodded. "Sometime during the early 1900s. We figure 1906 or so, according to the few records we've found. The hotel itself was built in 1896, originally to house workers for the sapphire mines. When London folk started buying up mining land a few years later, that section was added for household help. We use the room below it for laundry facilities now." Turning to the back wall, Betty pulled a key from one of the square cubbyholes and handed it to Paige.

"I put out coffee in the morning around seven. If you're a breakfast-type person, there's a little café down the road called Moonglow. Odd little place. Run by a hippie girl who paints watercolor landscapes. She moved out here from Santa Cruz. You know, California." Betty shrugged her shoulders. "She's kind of a strange person, but she sure knows how to cook. Serves lunch, too. Only takes cash, but there's an ATM halfway down the block."

"What about dinner?" Paige asked. The talk of food made her realize she hadn't eaten since her plane flight.

Betty shook her head. "Not much here in the evening. Everything closes up around 7 p.m., some places even at 6. If you need anything later than that, the closest place is about nine miles down the road at Wild Bill's."

"Wild Bill's?" Paige raised her eyebrows. The name conjured up a variety of images.

"Oh, don't you worry," Betty laughed. "Wildest thing that ever goes on in there is the waitress yelling at the cook to hurry up with an order. And that's not very often, seeing as customers are few and far between."

Stifling a yawn, Paige decided settling in for the night was more appealing than a nine-mile drive. A granola bar would have to suffice. In the morning she could make up for it at...what was that funny breakfast place called? Moonglow. She thanked Betty for her help and went up to her room.

It didn't take long to unpack her suitcase and hang her clothes in the antique walnut wardrobe that served as a closet. She'd packed light, checking only one bag with the airline, all casual clothes, plus a few sweaters. In addition, she'd worn a heavy coat on the plane, keeping it folded and on her lap for most of the trip. A carry-on bag held her laptop, notepaper and miscellaneous items ranging from toiletries to snacks.

Paige sat on the bed and settled back against the floral shams, fatigue from the long day of travel catching up to her. Even if she'd been in the mood for a full dinner, she wouldn't have had the energy to eat it. Checking email could wait until morning. She was tempted to call Jake, but she was sure she'd fall asleep on the phone, so that could wait as well. She used what felt like her last bit of strength to change into a nightshirt, fold down the quilted bedcovers and sink into the soft pillows, an area travel magazine spread open across her chest as her eyes closed.

CHAPTER THREE

Beneath the hotel's soft comforter, Paige awakened shivering. The crisp morning air stung her face. Half asleep, she pulled her body into a fetal position and tucked her head under the covers. This wasn't enough. She tried breathing out forcefully, hoping her warm breath would delay her inevitable departure from the bed. A few choice words tumbled from her lips. She'd fallen into bed without thinking to turn on the heater. Now she was paying the price.

Still cursing, she slid out from under the bedcovers. A rush of chilly air wrapped its fingers around her bare shoulders and crawled up her neck; she shuddered. She pulled a woven afghan from the foot of the bed and wrapped it around her. Better, but not by much.

She tiptoed to the window, chastising herself. She'd never developed an affinity for socks or slippers. The throw rug alongside the bed kept the first steps tolerable, but the slick wooden boards beyond were like sheets of ice against the soles of her feet. Her breath fogged up the glass pane immediately, giving her just a few seconds to see the frost on the roofing outside. Temperature in the low 30s was her best guess. She pulled the afghan more snugly around her body and buried her chin in the knitted bundle her hands grasped.

She searched the wall near the light switch, but found no trace of a thermostat. A check along the floorboards for heaters also proved useless. Her teeth were chattering by the time she finally saw an ancient radiator alongside the far wall. Approaching it quickly, she dropped to her knees and fumbled around, running her hands over the cold metal in search of a way to turn it on. Eventually she felt a round knob protruding from the far side. She twisted the round dial as forcefully as she could. It took a few tries, but it finally turned. A soft clicking gave her hope for warmth soon.

She held her hands out in front of the metal spirals and waited for heat. At first there was nothing, but then slight warmth began to radiate out. Or did it? Tempted to jump back into bed, she waited, letting her hands hover expectantly. She reached behind the radiator to check for warmth from the wall-facing side, but felt only cold air. She sighed. A one-sided radiator would take ages to heat the room.

Her knowledge of antique heating methods was sketchy. She'd lived in modern housing with central heat all her life. A twist of a thermostat control was all it had ever taken for her to warm up a cold room. Now she found herself examining the metal contraption in front of her like a sculptor might assess a block of clay, pulling here, pushing there.

She leaned over, inspecting the back again, still seeing nothing attached to the heating unit. Yet, a square of peeling wallpaper caught her attention. That was it, she thought, her confidence growing. A switch must control the radiator, enclosed behind a decorative wallpapered panel.

Pressing herself against the wall, she slid her hand along its surface, twisting her body in order to feel for a discrepancy in texture. Her fingers felt a rough edge of wallpaper that had separated from the panel next to it. She slipped her fingers underneath, expecting to feel a switch. Instead, she felt an unsteady block of wood. Changing positions, she inspected the area with her other hand. The unstable section shifted again. She adjusted her body once more and tried to pry the loose panel forward with her fingers. After several unsuccessful attempts, the wood gave way, revealing a cavity in the wall.

Paige's investigative nature was a near-compulsion, especially when she felt she was on the edge of a discovery, so despite visions of an expensive repair bill looming, she explored the interior of the wall with her fingers. Half-expecting an unpleasant encounter with spiders or termites, she was grateful to find these fears ungrounded. But she caught her breath anyway at the unexpected feel of leather against her fingertips.

The room's temperature forgotten, Paige worked her way around the object, feeling a smooth surface, with light scratches. A sharper texture followed that–wrinkled paper, barely attached to the leather. Her anticipation grew. Determined, she grasped one edge and pulled it forward, trying to remove it from the cavity. It resisted. Repeatedly, she tried to extricate it. Yet each time she adjusted her angle, the wall blocked its removal. Holding the object with one hand, she tried to enlarge the hole by pulling on the adjoining wall panel. Even another inch might do the trick. But the solid wall would not budge. She maneuvered the object again, hoping to adjust the angle so it would fit through the opening. Still no luck.

She adjusted her stance and used her body weight to pull harder. The increased force helped some. Half of the object protruded from the wall, while the rest remained wedged securely inside. When she slid her fingers behind the leather, she realized crumpled pages were loosely attached. It was a diary and, from the looks and feel of it, it had been enclosed in the wall for a while.

She braced one foot against the wall and clung to the diary securely, pulling back with the weight of her body. To her delight, she felt the book move forward. But to her dismay, a rough, tearing sound accompanied the motion. A hollow thud echoed from inside the wall as she fell backwards onto the floor.

Paige held the fragile notebook and blew lightly across its surface. Dust motes floated out into the chilly room. She blinked, to keep the dust from her eyes, and rubbed her nose to block a reflexive sneeze. Setting the tattered, partial book to the side, she pushed herself up off the floor and reached inside the wall, hoping to find the remaining pages wedged against a crossbeam or caught on a nail. Nothing. The rest of the old diary had fallen beyond her reach.

She retreated to the warmth of the bed, wrapped the afghan around her and slid as far under the covers as possible. Only a portion of her face and the hands holding the notebook remained exposed to the chilly air.

The cover was dull, brown leather, slightly scratched, but otherwise in good condition. Stitches held the pages together, at least the few warped sheets still attached. The notebook as a whole measured around four by six inches. It was impossible to estimate its depth in view of the missing pages. A ragged tear ran from the upper edge of the binding to the bottom.

A sharp ping caused Paige to jump, until she recognized the origin of the sound. The radiator was starting to work itself up. As were her nerves. Holding the book in her hands, she had the childlike sensation of being caught doing something she shouldn't be doing. Feeling foolish, she realized she had glanced over her shoulder at the sound.

Paige opened the notebook, taking care not to damage the faded pages. The faint initials "SW" were neatly penned inside the front cover. Dust drifted downward as she turned from one page to the next. Words in tiny penmanship filled page after page. At times the lettering was neat and precise. At other times it appeared scrawled and agitated. Raw emotions seemed to burst off the paper like flames, all depending upon the handwritten scroll of the text.

Paige was pleased the entries were dated. She turned first to the front page, then leafed through interior pages and, finally, scanned the last page that still clung to the ripped binding. Several years passed between the entries. Enough time to document something in detail – the development of the town, perhaps, or the history of the old hotel.

Thoughts of the room's chilly temperature disappeared as Paige focused on the notebook. She flipped to a random page and scanned a few lines.

Oct 24, 1922

C. has insulted me again. Is it my fault that Running Fox was not wearing red the last time he rode through here on that horse of his? I see what I'd like to see, not necessarily what is there. Realism? It's what's in my mind's eye that matters. He says my brush strokes lack vigor. It is paint, not electricity! I am a poor student, C. repeats over and over again. It's not true; I lack only his belief in me. More likely, he is a poor teacher and can't admit it.

Paige paused and glanced back at the newly exposed cavity in the wall before returning to the bound pages in her hands. Perhaps a child, based on the reference to being a student, kept the fragile notebook. Then again, the penmanship was an adult's, at least the passages that were neatly executed. The scrawled entries might indicate an elderly person, or maybe someone with occasional tremors. There was no way to know without reading further. Paige didn't need an invitation. She thumbed back to the first page and started in.

November 17, 1921

I am growing tired of not getting the recognition I deserve. C. is applauded everywhere he goes. One would think he creates each aspect of the actual scenes, not just the images. Does he give birth to the horses themselves? Of course not! He merely combines tints and hues and canvas, yet is accorded the respect of the Good Lord Himself. It's absurd adoration and not in the least bit merited. I have had superb education and speak properly. I dare say my talent exceeds his. Yes, C. has exhibited in London, but we have no royalty in the West. Why should he receive such praise here? I grow weary of sitting by while all roads lead to C.

April 4, 1922

I've been studying with C. for two years now. He is never pleased with me and it is high time I receive recognition of my own. I do believe he would like me to quit. Utter nonsense! What sort of a man does he think I am? Does he have a right to decide what my life should be? I hardly think so!

September 10, 1922

C. finished a new painting last week. It is striking, admittedly, with blue tones as deep as local sapphires and red specks the color of late sunset. What rage a piece like this stirs up in me! Is this really talent? Perhaps it is simply luck. I toil as hard, if not harder, yet his paintings are more vibrant. I will never give him the satisfaction of admitting it to his face.

Paige arrived at the entry she'd first scanned and flipped past it. The following two pages were illegible, one blurred – spilled coffee, perhaps, from the brown tint of the smudge – and the other, a short passage obliterated by sharp, manic X's, as if the writer had been so angry at his own words that he'd attempted to stab the page into oblivion. Why not just tear it out, Paige wondered. Was the process of creating, then destroying, therapeutic somehow? Or could the frustrated hands that spewed the words and slashes onto the pages simply be those of a man consumed with rage? Whether due to lack of recognition, lack of talent or simply the inability to convey his messages clearly, the writer's fury was undeniable.

A childhood memory hit Paige out of the blue, an early sign of the perfectionism she'd fought all of her life. She'd written a composition for elementary school. It was only a page long, but hand-written and single-spaced. Always slow and cautious with her printing, it had taken a good part of an hour to transcribe it from note cards. On the last line, she'd misspelled a word. Correcting it in pen, changing "n" to "m," it looked crowded, imperfect. In tears, Paige had torn up the paper and started from scratch. It would not be the only time she did that throughout her years of schooling.

The radiator rumbled. Paige turned the destroyed pages over and secured them under her left thumb. She moved her attention to the next page, dated almost a full year after the last one that had been legible. The lettering on this particular entry was precise and controlled, compared to others. If written letters themselves could be described as haughty, that was the appearance these gave. Had they been typed, they would have merely formed angry words. But the physical strokes of the hand that wrote them gave them emotionally charged life.

August 26, 1923

    I've been thrown out of C's studio. He has refused to give me future lessons, claiming that he's taught me everything he could. His pseudo-attempts to be kind while informing me of this were pitiful. He does not recognize my talent and clearly views me as a waste of his precious time. Must he also be so prolific? How selfish of him! He seeks only fame, while I seek true artistry. I loathe him.

Only three entries remained, dated years later, with long lapses in time between each.

October 26, 1926

    I hear word that C. has departed this earth. I suppose I should feel sadness, but not an ounce courses through me. What more could an artist ask for, other than what he achieved? And now he is gone. Well, of course, that's the natural order of things. I shed no tears.

February 26, 1937

    I attempted the simplest of scenes today, a lone Blackfoot atop a horse on a hill, overlooking this glorious Judith Basin. My intention was there, but the inspiration was not. The hills evolved dull and lifeless and the Blackfoot, without expression. In a fit worthy of a child of three, I kicked the easel and sent the piece soaring through the air. It landed against the wall, the sharp spike of a hook ripping through its fabric, leaving the frame rocking back and forth, taunting me. With defiant hands, I seized it and smashed it on the ground, finishing off its demolition with my work boots. Of course I felt no satisfaction whatsoever.

Dec. 23, 1942

Dreary winter times, void of color and inspiration. There is little to put on canvas and even less to put on paper.

Automatically, Paige turned the last page and looked for another, discouraged to find only a blank page and nothing attached beyond that. Any entries written after December 1942 were likely trapped inside the wall.

Cursing herself for yanking the book from the wall so carelessly, Paige tossed off the afghan and covers, ignoring the remaining chill in the room. She struggled once more to explore the inner cavity with her hand. With the radiator throwing off heat now, she had to avoid pressing against it, for fear of burning her skin. This resulted in even more contortions than before. Several times her arm became stuck inside the wall. To her relief, each time she was able to remove it. Common sense won out, and she surrendered. She would have to find another way to search. The rest of the diary was sure to have fallen. The first floor of the hotel would be the next place to look.

CHAPTER FOUR

The girl behind the counter was not what Paige expected, even with Betty's description from the evening before. She was tall and thin and moved with a subtle, gliding motion that should have been calming, but Paige found unsettling. She didn't look Californian – whatever that might mean. Her skin was pale, almost pasty, and her dusky hair – the portions not tied up above her head with a peacock feather – fell in wisps around her shoulders. She was a mouse, but too tall, a gazelle, but too slow. Her clothing struck Paige as odd in a way that she couldn't pinpoint, from the ivory gauze blouse tucked into a multi-colored, floral skirt to the work boots she might very well have inherited from a Cal Trans worker along a California highway. A lengthy earring of tiny seashells dangled from one ear lobe; in the other ear she wore nothing at all. For no logical reason, Paige felt nervous as the curious figure drew near.

"My name is Mist," the girl said, barely smiling. She stood before Paige's table, looking neither eager nor reluctant and continued to stand quietly until Paige spoke.

"Mist, that must be short for Misty," Paige said awkwardly.

"No," the girl responded. She gazed past Paige.

"Well, maybe for Mystique then, or Melissa," Paige offered.

"It's just Mist," the girl said and waited.

"I'd love a cup of coffee, please." Paige quickly realized it was best to stick to the business of a morning meal. The conversation was clearly going nowhere.

"Moonglow has Java Love," the girl said quietly. "It is not just coffee; it is love. It is the right way to start a new day."

"Java Love it is, then," Paige agreed. "One cup of Java Love." Anything to get the dose of caffeine started. It had been much easier getting a cup of coffee the morning before at JFK Airport.

"Java Love is not measured in cups. Java Love is limitless because love is limitless."

The girl pivoted away. Paige watched as she crossed the floor and entered the kitchen. After a few moments of muffled noise from the back, a carafe of coffee landed on her table, along with a thick pottery mug with a mottled glaze. Apparently Java Love, though limitless, could be consumed in measured amounts, by the mug full. Paige found this reassuring. She poured a generous amount of the fresh brew and took a sip. It was extraordinarily good.

"Will you want breakfast?"

The coffee was so exceptional that Paige had forgotten the unusual server still stood beside the table.

"Yes," she answered. "I'll take a look at a menu, thank you."

"Moonglow does not have menus. Menus complicate life. Today is Tuesday. I will bring your Tuesday breakfast. Is there anything that you do not or cannot eat?"

Paige wrapped both hands around the warm mug. "Anything is fine."

Again Mist retreated to the kitchen. Paige took another sip of coffee, followed by a pause, followed by a full gulp. She was still on New York time and New York momentum. Reentry to the slower pace of the West was going to be rough for a couple of days. The caffeine was helping.

Paige stood and wandered around the empty dining room, taking the mug of coffee with her. Soft-hued paintings of landscapes hung at varying heights on the walls. Golden tones of rolling hillsides blended in with the natural wooden walls of the café. Blue watercolor skies picked up the sparkle of dangling crystals in the front windows. A tiny, flowing "M" had been added to the lower right hand corner of each piece. Betty had mentioned that Mist painted, but she hadn't said how talented the girl was.

Paige returned to her seat just as Mist placed an oblong plate on the table. Aromas of apples, cinnamon and fresh cream floated up from a magazine-perfect presentation of breakfast fare. Papaya slices and blackberries lined the left side of the plate, forming an edging to what seemed to be a cross between an apple pancake and cinnamon pudding, topped with whipped cream and a drizzle of maple syrup. She took a bite of frittata to the right of the sweet entrée. The blend of spinach, sun-dried tomatoes and feta cheese was perfection. Any thoughts of a rough first day vanished as she savored the meal.

When finished, Paige set the plate aside gently, almost reverently, took a few more slow sips of coffee and asked for the bill.

"Leave what your heart tells you. You are ready for the day now," Mist replied, removing the plate and vanishing once again into the kitchen, leaving Paige at a loss. When she didn't reappear, Paige stood and left a generous amount of cash. As she was leaving the café, a group of five or six people, chatting and laughing, entered Moonglow. *Good,* Paige thought as she walked back to the hotel. *She's a little daffy, but she deserves the business.*

"I can tell you've been to Moonglow and have met Mist," Betty said as Paige stepped into the hotel. "You've got that glimmer that says you're ready for the day."

"I'm sure I overpaid," Paige said.

"We all do," Betty laughed. "If Mist ever leaves, we'll be stuck with Wild Bill's."

At the front desk, Paige picked up a map of the town, unfolded it and placed it on the counter. It was designed for tourists, with lines indicating streets and whimsical drawings that represented town businesses or sightseeing spots. The name "Timberton," was written across the top in a lavish script with a scroll sketched in the background. The entire map served more as artwork and advertising than function, but it worked for Paige's purpose.

"Off to explore?" Betty asked while dusting a Tiffany-style lamp at the end of the counter.

Paige nodded. "I need to make a couple phone calls and then head over to the gem store you have in this town. I'm researching sapphire mining for *The Manhattan Post* and figure that's a good place to start."

Betty nodded without much enthusiasm. "You're talking about The Timberton Gem Gallery. I doubt you'll find much out there. The shop's a tourist attraction, something to draw people into Timberton and bring the town a little income. They sell gravel by the scoopful, which people buy up and sort through, hoping to find special stones, sapphires in particular. You'll see pictures on the wall of gems that have supposedly been found by customers. Whether that's true or not, I don't know."

"Can't hurt to take a look." Paige tried to stay optimistic though her hopes of digging up much information in this town were sinking. "It's a starting place."

"That it is," Betty agreed. "Probably the only place in town *to* start, for that matter. At least you'll get an earful of fanciful stories, if nothing else. Clive Barnes runs that store, and he's lived here his whole life. Old curmudgeon, that one," Betty grumbled.

"I'll remember that." Paige laughed as she headed upstairs to get her cell phone.

She needed to make two calls. The first would be easy, just a quick call to touch base with Susan and let her know she'd made it to Timberton. The second call made her nervous, ridiculous as it seemed. She'd jumped at the opportunity Susan offered by packing quickly, booking the room at the Timberton Hotel and heading straight to Montana. What she hadn't done was to warn Jake that she was on her way out west. Whether to surprise him or out of her own hesitation, she'd decided to wait until she was in Timberton to contact him about her trip. After all, it wasn't as if she were dropping directly into his town without notice. Timberton was easily an eight-hour drive from Jackson, Wyo. Logistically, it was possible they wouldn't even be able to see each other, though that thought depressed her.

Oddly enough, glimmers of insecurity had started to haunt her. It was one thing to meet and form an attachment for a few weeks, as they had done on her previous trip. And keeping in touch during the following weeks had seemed natural. Every few days one of them had called the other, chatting casually about daily news and sidestepping any heavier conversation. They hadn't discussed specifics about when they might see each other again.

Paige refocused her attention on work and dialed the number to *The Manhattan Post*, entering the extension for Susan's office. It went straight to voicemail, a reminder that she was two hours behind New York time. While she had just finished a leisurely breakfast, her editor would already be headed out to an early lunch meeting.

After leaving a brief message, Paige disconnected the call and dialed Jake's number, which also went to voicemail. She left a brief, casual hello. She could surprise him with her whereabouts when he returned her call.

Paige slipped the cell phone into a pocket of her jeans and headed back downstairs. Betty had finished dusting and was now tackling the floorboards with a broom.

"Where will I find The Timberton Gem Gallery?" Paige asked as she crossed the entryway and peered out a leaded glass window. She looked up and down the street.

"You can't see it from here," Betty said. "It's about two blocks down, on this side, on the corner of Main Street and Gulch Road. You'll know it when you see it, what with its gaudy storefront and all. A real eyesore, in my opinion." Betty sighed and shook her head.

"Not your style, Betty?" Paige asked, amused.

"Not anyone's style, if you ask me," Betty answered. "Clive has no idea how a real business should look. He wouldn't even have customers if it weren't for people thinking they might end up with a gem straight out of a fairy tale. Of course, they just go away disappointed."

"Well, maybe I'll be the lucky one who takes a two carat stone home with me." Paige said as she headed for the door.

Betty's laughter followed her. "Go for four carats, as long as you're dreaming."

CHAPTER FIVE

A walk along Timberton's Main Street revealed that the gem gallery wasn't the only tourist-oriented business. One after another, weathered structures housed shops filled with western garb, jewelry and souvenirs. Old wooden barrels and milk jugs lined the boarded sidewalks, a few filled with shrubbery. Window displays were upscale, aimed at visitors looking to spend some cash while traveling. Timberton didn't appear to be much more than a tourist stop.

Paige smiled as she passed "Pop's Parlor." No western town would be complete without a saloon. The door stood ajar and country music poured out. The bar was just getting revved up for the day. An old-fashioned candy store followed, looking oddly out of place next door to a bar. After Paige passed a few more boutiques, she reached the gem gallery.

Betty hadn't exaggerated. In contrast to the chic style of the other shops, the gem gallery was tacky. A false front, painted in harsh, primary shades of red and blue, reached higher than the surrounding buildings. Christmas lights hung across the frontage, draped unevenly. Two thirds of the lights glared brightly. The other third were burned out. The *pièce de resistance* was a life-sized cutout of a miner that protruded from the roof at an angle. Paige stepped out from under it, worried that the shaky plank of wood could fall at any minute.

Garish yellow painted words on the front windows' glass panes beckoned tourists in with promises of treasure. Someone had taped up pictures of proud customers displaying their sparkling discoveries. Another row of haphazard lights lined the doorway. Betty was right; the place was gaudy. Paige would even call it downright ugly.

When Paige stepped inside, she was surprised to find the gallery itself was tasteful and appealing. It consisted mostly of unpainted wooden walls and rustic support posts. An antique glass case displayed polished gems set in 14k gold pendants and rings. Customers would probably assume that the jewelry held locally mined gems, though Paige questioned the gems' true origins. Nothing about the place felt authentic.

Her opinion didn't matter; she was there to research the area's mining history. Tourist trap or not, the gallery was her only alternative to Google for researching the topic.

"You're looking at authentic Yogo sapphires! Nothing prettier 'n that."

She jumped at the sound of the nearby voice.

"Are you Clive?"

"In the flesh!"

Clive Barnes looked exactly as Paige had imagined him. He was of medium height and slight, easily in his mid-70s. Dressed in overalls, a faded red shirt and sporting a bandana around his neck, he looked like a movie character. Scuffed work boots with tattered, leather laces completed the look. Paige could see he'd been a Timberton fixture his entire life.

"I've been running this gallery most of my life," Clive said, as if he'd read Paige's mind. "I've seen many a sparkling sapphire in my time, and helped a lot of others find them, too. I bet there's one here just waiting for you to discover it."

He nodded his head toward a worktable and tapped his finger against the jewelry case at the same time.

"You've got a beautiful assortment here," Paige said. It was an impressive collection of sapphires. The center of the case held elegant rings, sparkling pendants and shimmering earrings, all mounted with differing sizes and shapes of stones. "The settings are beautiful, so unique. I've never seen anything like them."

Clive looked pleased. "Thank you kindly, ma'am. I like to think of myself as a designer, gives me something to do in my spare time. There's a lot of that around here lately – spare time, that is."

Paige was stunned. "You designed these?"

"Yep. One-of-a-kind. I just keep making them so folks coming through Timberton have a chance to take home a sparkling bit of Montana that can't be found anywhere else. One of these bracelets would look mighty fine on that slender wrist of yours." He motioned to the arm Paige had extended alongside the display. Her fingertips brushed the oak trim of the jewelry case.

Paige resisted the urge to laugh. He had his pitch down pat. Whether it was true or not that he'd led visitors to discover gems, she didn't doubt that he'd gotten many of them to try. And if they didn't find anything, there was always the display case. For the right price, they could take home a showy souvenir.

"You're that New York reporter, I bet," Clive said. "I heard you were coming out to pay our little town a visit."

"Word travels quickly," Paige said. "I only found out myself a couple days ago."

"Modern times, fast communication. Besides, I've had a few jewelers from back east calling, lately, looking to get ahold of some sapphires right quick. Some sort of gem convention coming up, right?"

Paige nodded. Businesses were always looking to make money off of convention attendees. It was natural to hear jewelers were making calls. "Exactly," Paige said. "The paper I work for is planning to run an article on Montana sapphire mining."

"Well, you've come to the right place, then. Who knows," Clive raised his eyebrows, "you just might end up with a nine carat dazzler like the one Prince Charles gave Lady Diana Spencer as an engagement ring."

"Princess Diana's ring?" It sounded far-fetched.

Clive shrugged. "Well, that's what they said for a long time. Nowadays most people think that was just a legend. Sounds impressive, though, don't you think?"

"Impressive, but not likely," Paige said. "Montana's quite a ways from England." She leaned over the display case, noticing the soothing blue tone to many of the sapphires, not as dark as others she'd seen. Not that she'd ever paid much attention to precious gems. Jewelry had never been an obsession of hers, unless it had sentimental value. She reached up and fingered the gold locket that dangled from a dainty chain around her neck, a gift from Jake.

"More likely than you'd think," Clive said. "These sapphires were mined by the English for many years during the early 1900s. Charles Gadsen ran those operations, and plenty of stones made their way across the Atlantic. He knew what he was doing, putting in mine shafts and timber supports inside all that limestone and then waiting for nature to take its course. You can't blast those crystals out without fracturing them. It takes weathering to bring them out."

"So *these* are Yogos." Paige said. "Are they called Yogos because of the color? It's an unusual blue, not what I think of as sapphire blue."

"They're from Yogo Gulch, that's why the name. And that cornflower blue is one of their claims to fame. They're not all that color, but the ones that are shine like the blue Montana sky. Big, blue skies we have out here, you know."

Paige glanced at the display case again. "You've got a couple rubies in here too, it looks like."

"Actually, those are sapphires, too. Not all sapphires are blue. It depends on their mineral concentration. You get chromium in there, you get red crystals."

"And the blue?" Paige pulled a notepad and pen from her purse. She clicked the pen several times before starting to jot down notes.

"Iron and titanium," Clive said. "It's not quite that simple, but that's the short version."

Paige wandered toward the work area. Raised strips of wood formed a short barrier around a large worktable. Piles of gravel sat in haphazard clusters.

"Are all Montana sapphires Yogos?" Paige set her notepad on the table and leaned over it, continuing to write.

"Nope," Clive answered. "Yogo Gulch isn't the only sapphire deposit in the state. They come from the Rock Creek, Missouri River and Dry Cottonwood Creek mines, too. But Yogos are unique. Tiffany & Co. called them 'sapphires of unusual quality.' A mountain man named Jake Hoover sent them a box of pebbles in 1894."

Paige stopped her note taking at the sound of the name. She still hadn't heard back from *her* Jake. Maybe she could reach him that evening unless he called her first. She refocused her attention and resumed writing.

"Imagine," Clive continued, "back then all anyone cared about was finding gold. Most miners just tossed the blue pebbles aside. They'd get stuck in the sluice boxes, and prospectors considered them a nuisance. That Hoover fellow was a smart one. Tiffany & Co. sent him a check for $3,750. Quite a bit of money in those days."

"Nothing to sneeze at today, either." Paige ran a few expenses through her mind that a few thousand dollars could cover.

"They'd bring a lot more now," Clive said. "Yogos fetch a good price. They're strong, and their color is natural. They don't need heat-treatment like other sapphires do. And they don't have the inclusions that stones from other areas have."

"Inclusions?" Paige questioned.

"Flaws. Feathers, pinpoints, carbons, other kinds. Inclusions can affect the transmission of light. Or they can weaken the stone itself, if they're near the surface. They're very common and not a problem if small. But the fact that they're rare in Yogos adds to the value of these particular gems."

Clive stepped around the worktable and spread out one of the piles of pebbles. The sweep of his arm had a dramatic flair to it, and Paige knew it was an attempt to entice her into a hunt for sapphires.

"Not today, Clive," Paige said. Disappointment spread across his face. "Maybe before I leave Timberton."

"There's a pretty gem waiting in here for you, I just know it." Even Clive had to smile at his obvious sales pitch. He gathered the pebbles back into a pile again and walked Paige to the door. She thanked him for the brief lesson and headed back to the hotel.

A breeze had kicked up while Paige was inside the gallery, and a small funnel of dust blew up in her face as she crossed the road. She stepped back inside the boardwalk and took shelter against the wall of the candy store, pulling out her cell phone again to check for messages. Still no return call from Jake. She was disappointed and even more dismayed to admit it to herself. Where was the independent city girl?

Paige fumbled around in her purse, running her fingers through the loose change that always seemed to accumulate at the bottom. Pulling out a handful of quarters, she dropped six into a sidewalk vending machine, caught a diet soda as it rolled into the lower tray. She sat down on a nearby bench.

Dealing with relationships had never been her strength. She was stubborn and work driven, always had been. While college friends had been out dating and partying, she'd put her energy into developing a career path. Their lifestyles had seemed frivolous to her, a waste of time. Her choice had seemed to work for Paige. She'd gone on to grad school and right into a journalism internship. Admittedly, she'd been wistful at some of their bridal showers and weddings, but not when the first divorce or two came around.

Paige leaned back against the bench and lifted the soda to her mouth, feeling the sizzle of carbonation as it made its way down her throat. She lowered the bottle and glanced up as a metal, rackety noise attracted her attention. A silver glint of sunlight bounced off a wobbling hubcap whisked along by the wind.

Across the street, an elderly man rested on a park bench. Paige mistook him at first for a statue, the type often found in tourist locations. An old miner perhaps, appropriate for Timberton visitors. When he unfolded his arms, he knocked down that theory. He was definitely alive. Quiet, but alive. Paige estimated his age to be at least eighty.

"Don't mind our local homeless guy." Betty's voice startled Paige so much that she almost dropped the soda. She turned to find the hotelkeeper about to step into the candy store.

"Gotta have caramels," Betty said, as simply as one might allude to taking daily vitamins. She disappeared inside, reappearing a few minutes later with a small bag. She mumbled a few words, undoubtedly testing out the product.

"He's been coming here for years, spring and summer. Stays in a shelter up in Utica during winter months, I think," Betty said with a slight smack. "Never says a word. Just sits in the same spot, changes positions now and then. Pokes that stick around in the dirt, sometimes picks up pebbles and puts them in his pockets."

Betty folded down the top edge of the bag and pushed the remaining caramels into her coat pocket. "Clive Barnes followed him one night after he closed up shop. Found him down by the Timberton Trestle. People have tried talking to him about getting a place to live, but they get no response. He doesn't bother anyone, so we just let him be."

"Does anyone know his name?"

"Nope, we just call him Hollister." Betty succumbed to temptation and pulled another caramel from her pocket, crinkling the edge of the bag in the process. "He wears a shirt that says Hollister on it, so we went with that. At least the last few months. Used to be Calvin."

Paige smiled. Hollister, a popular clothing line. Of course. And Calvin Klein before that, which sounded oddly out of place in a western town.

"There's a thrift shop here in Timberton, I bet," Paige said.

Betty beamed. "Yes, there is. A mighty fine one, too, Second Hand Sadie's. I found the prettiest purple sweater there last year, fluffy and soft, with little pearl buttons. I try to check in there every couple weeks. Tourists drop things off to lighten their suitcases on the way home. Make room for souvenirs. Why do you ask?"

"Just a wild guess," Paige said, smiling. She took another sip of soda and politely declined a caramel.

"You've got some characters in this town."

Betty chortled. "Oh, my, yes we do. We certainly do. Take Sadie, for example. She's a tiny little thing, barely 100 pounds. Pale skin, soft, gray hair and wire-rimmed glasses - reminds me of a baby bird. But you don't dare try to argue with her. If she says a hat costs $3, you'd better not offer $2.99. I heard she chased Ernie out of the thrift store with a broom a few weeks ago just because he asked for 50 cents off an old wooden barrel. And if she forgets your name – which happens all the time, by the way – you just go with whatever she calls you that day. I was Gertie last Monday and might be Hannah next Thursday."

"Who's Ernie?"

"Oh, he's the night bartender at Pop's Parlor, right there." Betty nodded her head toward the saloon's entrance. "Nice guy, but he's about three times Sadie's size. Used to play football up in Missoula. It must've been quite a sight watching that tiny woman chase him. Wish I could've seen it with my own two eyes, but I heard about it the last time I had my hair done at the Curl 'N Cue."

"Did you say Curly Q?" Paige asked.

"No, I sure didn't," Betty said. "Our little beauty shop is called the Curl 'N Cue because it's backed up onto Pop's Parlor. You can get yourself a nice perm and then walk right on through to the billiards room behind the bar."

Betty laughed and shook her head. "Yep, we've sure got our share of characters here in Timberton. And that's a good thing, I reckon. Keeps life interesting."

CHAPTER SIX

Paige stood up and moved away from the writing desk in her room. She was having a terrible time organizing her notes from her interview with Clive. Her cell phone remained silent, and her voicemail was empty. After a frustrated hour, she gave up trying to write, picked up the keys to her rented Hyundai and left the hotel.

Without a set destination, Paige chose one of the dusty, semi-paved roads that headed away from Timberton. She'd left Bozeman with a full tank of gas and had at least half a tank left. She could afford a bit of random driving.

The midday sun beat down on the car, counteracting the chill of the late fall air. Paige could find nothing on the car radio that was static free or even vaguely interesting, so she opted for silence. She adjusted the visor and opened her window an inch so that the slight breeze would help keep her alert. Comfortable, she eased back against the car's seat and let her mind wander as she drove.

Timberton was an odd town. Maybe she had expected something different, something more western. Or larger. Whatever she had expected, this wasn't it. It was not at all what she'd consider a typical tourist trap. A few of its buildings dated back to the old days, but with newer structures mixed in. Most had been built to resemble the old buildings, but not in any cohesive overall arrangement. The town was just not as remarkable as she wanted it to be.

The people of Timberton were another thing altogether. She'd arrived barely twenty-hours ago, and her list of acquaintances read like something from *The Twilight Zone*. First there was Betty, the carbon copy of Andy Griffith's Aunt Bee, with her caramel-smacking chatter and the spruced up interior – yet fading exterior – of her hotel. Clive Barnes was fresh out of a used car commercial, though clad in miners' garb – a costume for the part. Strange as the other various townsfolk were, from the feisty thrift storeowner to the mute man everyone called Hollister, they were no match in oddity for Mist, who did not fit Timberton at all. The new age flower child, as well as her Moonglow café, added an almost extraterrestrial element to the already bizarre town.

A metallic clang interrupted Paige's thoughts and shushed the silent sci-fi music accompanying the lineup of Timberton's townsfolk running through her mind. Paige pulled the little car over to the side of the road to inspect it. She could find no damage. All four tires seemed solid; there were no scratches; and no fluids were draining on the ground. But it was a good reminder to take it slow on country roads.

Paige leaned against the car and pulled her cell phone out of her pocket to find she had no service. She'd have to wait to check voicemail. Surely Jake would have left a message by now. Susan was more likely to shoot back a quick email from work, but Jake wasn't much of an email type. He probably wouldn't even have a cell phone if he didn't feel he needed one for emergencies. He was a loner who spent most of his time at home. The ranch he had purchased the year before in Jackson Hole was more than enough to keep him busy. In buying a property that had been abandoned for decades, he had acquired not only a deed to the land, but also a lengthy list of needed repairs. Winter was coming fast. He'd been trying to do as much as possible before the snowy season arrived.

That could be any day now, Paige realized as the wind chilled her. She climbed back in the car, pausing before turning on the ignition. Should she continue on or go back to the hotel? It wasn't yet late afternoon, so she'd have plenty of light if she drove farther out of town.

In her rearview mirror, she saw flashing lights and the dusky paint of a sheriff's car. "Uh oh. What now?"

A stocky man stepped out of the official car, placed his hat on his head and came up to knock on her car window. She rolled it down.

"Is there a problem?"

"License and registration, Miss."

Paige pulled her wallet out of her purse and handed the man her license then searched through the glove box for the registration with no luck.

"I'm sorry. I'm not sure where the registration is. This is a rental car. Did I do something wrong?"

"New York City, huh?" The officer exaggerated a fake New York accent. He returned Paige's license. "No problem, Miss. I just wanted to make sure you weren't in trouble or lost. We do have tourists who find their way out of town but have trouble finding their way back in. Best you go on back to Timberton if that's where you were. Sun goes down quickly here so you think you have plenty of light but then – poof! Light's gone."

He was right. The sun did seem to set earlier in Montana than it did in New York. Maybe she had misjudged how much time she had. The scare with the clanking sound against the car, the lack of cell service and the officer's advice convinced her. She'd give up her explorations and go back to the hotel.

"Thank you for your concern, Officer..."

"Sheriff. Sheriff Myers. You be careful, Miss. I don't want to hear that I have to organize a search party for you." He touched the brim of his hat and left. Paige turned the car around and headed back to Timberton.

* * * *

As Paige stepped into the hotel, the sound of dishes clattering and scent of cookies baking greeted her. Instead of checking in with Betty, she slipped up the stairs and into her room so she could check her cell phone messages in private. Still no word from Jake. She stretched out on the bed and threw an arm across her forehead. She laughed at herself. What a dramatic gesture! Fatigue and jet lag, she rationalized - and, admittedly, disappointment. The anticipation of seeing Jake again had followed her across the country and was woven into her eagerness to pursue a new assignment. Now her enthusiasm was slipping on both fronts. Seeing Jake was beginning to look iffy, and getting a gripping story out of the weird little town wasn't looking much more likely. Were pretty, blue stones without - what were they called - inclusions enough to interest New York readers? Doubtful.

She was glad when a light tap on the door interrupted her pity party.

"Something for dessert later on," Betty said. She held a dainty, china plate with several warm chocolate chip cookies on it.

"Ah, one of my weaknesses," Paige sighed. She accepted the offering, set the plate on the nightstand and reached for a cookie.

"Don't go spoiling your appetite," Betty said. "Mist has whipped something up for dinner. You'll want to head over there around 6 or so."

"I thought Moonglow didn't serve dinner," Paige said. "It sounded like Wild Bill's was the only option. I was just thinking your fresh-baked cookies could get me through the night."

"Most nights that's true. But on Tuesdays, when Mr. Hodges is in town, Mist often cooks something up. No sense in passing up a Moonglow meal."

So I can be ready for the night, I suppose, Paige thought.

Before Paige could object, Betty turned and scurried down the hallway.

Ready for the day, ready for the night. Ready to head back to New York was more like it. She had to pin down an angle on the sapphires and get out of Dodge before she went crazy. She'd give herself two more days. She'd have to hope she could find anything else she needed on Google.

Paige sighed. As a polite guest, she knew she should go to dinner. As a discouraged reporter, it was the last thing she wanted to do. And she had to wait for an hour. Throwing on sweats, finding a good book in the hotel's common area and scarfing down cookies were the only things that sounded appealing. Instead, she dragged herself to the shower, letting the steaming water wash away both the Montana dust from the short afternoon road adventure and some of her negative attitude.

Forty-five minutes later, she felt better. Standing in front of the dresser's oval, antique mirror, she leaned forward and slipped on a pair of gold hoop earrings, brushed on a tiny bit of mascara and blush and raked her fingers through her still-damp hair. Stepping back, she had to admit she felt a surge of energy. She was overdressed for Timberton in slacks and a silky, hunter green turtleneck. But sprucing up had lifted her spirits. It was an old, unoriginal trick, but a hot shower and spiffy outfit were a better cure for the blues than sweats and cookies. The cookies and sweats could wait.

The sun had set, and it was almost pitch black when she stepped outside. The earlier chill had grown more severe. She buttoned the front of her jacket and buried her hands deep in the pockets. She wished she'd thought to pack gloves.

By the time she walked the short distance to Moonglow, Paige was freezing. The small café looked inviting. Candles glowed in the front windows, and others cast faint outlines along the pathway that led to the front door. The heated air began to thaw her as soon as she stepped inside.

As Paige removed her jacket and hung it on a peg by the door, she heard the soft music of Enya flowing through the dining room. The café's ambience was nothing like it had been at breakfast when the emphasis had been on energy and movement.

Tiny votive candles sat in the center of each table in tin holders. Star patterns created ethereal designs on the surrounding wooden surfaces. The tables themselves were different shapes and sizes. Had she noticed that this morning? Hanging at varied heights from the ceiling were paper lanterns, also star shaped. Where had she seen those before? She thought back. Ah, Ocracoke Island, another assignment, another time. What memories Moonglow called up. Strange, chameleon café. It was as if the interior of the restaurant changed according to the time and circumstance, wrapping itself around customers like a blanket.

Mist led Paige to a table. Paige was dismayed to see that another diner sat there already, hunched down behind an open newspaper. Of course, Mr. Hodges. So much for having a solitary meal and enjoying the magical atmosphere. She'd have to play the polite other guest from the hotel. Her mood plummeted. Not even Enya could help.

As she followed Mist and said hello, Paige wished she hadn't been raised to have good manners. Mr. Hodges remained buried behind the paper and didn't bother to return her greeting. Rude, she thought. If she'd wanted to dine with nothing more than a man's hat and a newspaper, she probably could have found that at Wild Bill's.

Mist materialized next to Paige and stood waiting. For lack of anything else to say, Paige asked for a glass of white wine.

"Whatever you recommend, Mist. I trust your judgment."

Pivoting in her "Mist manner," the café owner retreated to the kitchen without taking Mr. Hodges' drink order. Ha, Paige thought, serves him right for being so antisocial. Mist fixed dinner for him every Tuesday? She was a kind spirit, indeed.

Because of her breakfast experience, Paige knew better than to expect a menu. She looked around the room again. As her eyes grew accustomed to the candlelight, she began to make out the landscape paintings on the walls. In the dimness, the artwork looked abstract. Like the café itself, Paige thought, like Mist's universe.

To Paige's surprise, Mist reappeared and set a chilled flute of champagne in front of her; candlelight struck the sparkling bubbles. Lost in the warm glow, Paige reached for the glass, but her hand paused mid-air as she watched Mist place a second flute across the table and then set a long-stemmed red rose between the two. In a second, she knew what was happening.

"Jake," she whispered.

The newspaper fell to the table and Paige caught her breath. Jake was even more handsome than Paige remembered, all blue eyes, chiseled chin, deep tan and windswept hair. She had missed him. Now here he was, his sly grin revealing she was the recipient of a well-planned surprise.

"Hi, Paige," Jake said, looking pleased with himself.

"You tricky rascal! How?"

"First a toast. To Paige MacKenzie, intrepid reporter."

Paige lifted her own glass and clinked it against Jake's. "To Jake Norris, mysterious cowboy!" She took a sip of champagne before setting down her glass. "So, how did you pull this off?"

"Your office," Jake said. "I called there yesterday because I couldn't reach you on your cell phone."

"I was in flight. My phone was off. And you hate leaving messages, don't you?" Paige crossed her arms and tried to look annoyed. But she couldn't stop smiling.

"And you just go trouncing across the country, heading west, no less, without a word of warning." Jake's tone was 95 percent teasing and 5 percent scolding.

"I didn't have much notice, to tell the truth," Paige said. "Besides, I thought maybe I'd surprise you."

"Well, I do believe I beat you to it." Jake rocked back in his chair, looking like a schoolboy who'd just gotten away with an excellent prank.

"Yes, I believe you did."

Enya had moved seamlessly into a haunting blend of pan flutes and soft drums. Jake's eyes reflected candlelight. As Jake leaned forward and lowered his voice to a whisper, Paige gave in to the urge to touch his hand with light fingertips just to be sure she wasn't imagining his presence.

"Will we be getting menus soon?" Jake looked around the café for Mist. "I worked up an appetite driving today."

Paige slid her hand back to her champagne flute, leaned forward, too, and matched his secretive tone.

"Moonglow doesn't have menus," Paige whispered. "Menus complicate life." She felt a wave of satisfaction at Jake's puzzled look. He may have surprised her first, but at least she had a head start on knowing Timberton's quirks.

Two plates of food glided silently onto the table; the aromas of caramelized onions and port sauce rose up. Slender stalks of fresh asparagus fanned out to the left side of two tender, beef medallions. A diminutive, almond-encrusted puff pastry of baked Brie accompanied the meal. Jake looked at the plate and back up at Paige.

"Trust me," Paige said. "Just eat anything she serves. The breakfast I had this morning was heavenly. If I could, I'd eat every meal here for the rest of my life."

Jake dug into the gourmet meal, glancing around the café between bites. Paige watched him and knew he was as curious as she'd been since she arrived in Timberton. Hunger trumped conversation temporarily, but as he finished a last bite of Brie, he spoke.

"What kind of town is this, anyway? It didn't look like much when I drove in. But then the only café in town serves up a meal like this? I don't get it."

Paige could only agree.

"I wish I could tell you. It's an odd place, that's for sure." Paige paused as Mist switched out the empty dinner plates for two coffees, one miniature chocolate soufflé and two spoons.

"What does Susan have you working on this time?" Jake sipped his coffee

"I'm writing a sapphire article to coincide with a gemology convention coming up in New York in a few weeks," Paige said. "There's a gem gallery in town, and the owner knows a lot about Montana sapphire mining and the town's history. Once I get a good focus, I hope it won't take long to pull it together. But there's something else."

Jake took a sip of coffee as Paige lowered her voice again.

"I came across an old diary last night while I was trying to figure out how to turn on the heat in my room."

"One of those display pieces that hotels put out for guests to see?" Jake said, holding his coffee cup close to his face to breathe in the aroma. "Wow, this coffee is excellent."

"No," Paige said. "I mean, yes, the coffee is amazing, but no, the diary isn't a display piece. It was hidden inside the wall. I'm sure it belonged to a local artist. This town is filled with unusual characters and secrets," Paige said, dipping a spoon into the soufflé. "It seems surreal."

"Yes, I agree, surreal," Jake said. "What are the entries in this diary like? Do they have anything to do with sapphires?"

Paige looked a little guilty. "Nothing to do with sapphires. From what I've read so far, the diarist was a painting student who was frustrated with his teacher and his own work. He was an angry person, but his story intrigues me."

"Yes, I remember how you can't resist the possibility of a good story." Jake's voice had softened. He reached across the table and laced his fingers with Paige's. That simple contact unnerved but warmed her. It was good to feel his touch.

"How does a cool, Montana evening walk sound after we pay the tab?" Jake nodded to the café's front door.

"I wouldn't hold your breath waiting for a check," Paige laughed. "Payment for meals here is just as bizarre as everything else in this town."

"If we don't get a bill, how do we know what we owe?" Jake said. Paige guessed that nothing in Timberton made sense to Jake.

"To quote what Mist told me this morning, 'leave what your heart tells you.'"

"Well," Jake sighed, "My heart tells me I'd better appreciate an extraordinary meal when I have a chance." He stood and pulled out a worn, leather wallet from the back pocket of his jeans, taking several bills and dropping them on the table.

Just seeing Jake stand moved Paige to a familiar breathlessness. The scuffed boots were the same ones he'd been wearing when she'd first met him in Jackson Hole. The sound of his first step onto Moonglow's wooden floor brought back memories of a day in another café, one state away. Had it really been only a month? She admired the snug, relaxed fit of his jeans. They looked like the same jeans as before, though the belt buckle was different. It was similar to the silver buckles she'd seen him wear, but with a trace of gold edging. The design featured majestic mountains and pine trees that surrounded a rustic bridge.

"Like it?"

Paige blushed. She knew she'd stared at that belt buckle a bit too long. Of course she liked it. All of it. What was not to like about this Wyoming cowboy?

"Recent addition to your wardrobe?"

Jake grinned. "Even guys shop sometimes, you know." He helped her up from her chair, picked up the long-stemmed, red rose and presented it to her with a slight bow.

"Dramatic," she teased.

"Well, drama could be your middle name, if I recall your last visit correctly." Jake released her hand and slid his arm around her shoulders.

"Not this time." Paige sighed. They stepped out into the cold night and paused on the sidewalk. "The people are interesting, and the diary adds an intriguing twist, but there's not a drop of drama to be found in this town from what I can tell."

"That's fine," Jake said. "You're here to do an article on sapphires. Maybe the town's old-time residents will find the diary interesting. Anyway, the most important thing is that you're here." He turned Paige toward him and drew her close.

"I think maybe you should show me this diary," Jake whispered, his lips brushing Paige's ear. "You know…the one in your room?"

"Yes." Paige said with a soft smile. "I think that's a good idea."

CHAPTER SEVEN

Mist had grown used to the sharp click of the latch as she closed the front door behind her guests. If she had her way, there wouldn't be a latch at all on the door, nor on any of the windows. Locks kept people closed off when they should strive to remain open to each other. But she was only the business owner. When it came to the menu, she could follow any whim she desired. When it came to the building, she had the limits of any other tenant, and that meant locks on the doors.

Clive Barnes wasn't bad, as landlords went. He had seemed glad to find someone who was interested in renting the old café, which had been vacant for years and had fallen prey to transients and vandals. The relief in his voice had been clear when she had first called from California to ask about the place. He asked a fair price, more than fair, probably because the residents of Timberton were in dire need of a decent place to eat. The few other eateries within the town limits were open only during the summer season and closed their doors as soon as fall arrived and the tourists disappeared. And it seemed no one wanted to drive down the road to Wild Bill's.

It had all fallen into place perfectly. She'd researched every town and city in Judith Basin County, from Great Falls to Billings. This territory was home to one of the American West's finest painters: Charles Russell. She'd been enthralled with his work from the first day she began dabbling with painting techniques as an art student in Santa Cruz. His pieces were soft in color, yet bold with reality. They portrayed a life that was nothing like hers. Russell's images told stories of the Sioux and Blackfoot, not of California surfers. They represented tableaus of dry, open land, not the infinite waters of the Pacific Ocean. Yet they spoke to her.

She'd paid her way through art school by working at a beachside bistro, a tiny place with only a half dozen tables. Since there wasn't an opening for a server, she'd ended up in the kitchen prepping food for the cooks. Chopping vegetables seemed like the last thing that would interest her, but she found the repetitive motions soothing. When she began helping the chef prepare sauces, her interest grew more intense. She'd find herself daydreaming in art class, counting the minutes until class would end and she could go to work. The varying colors of the food, the textures and flavors of the sauces and, ultimately, the presentation of the final dishes, became her art. It was not long before she became the chef's right-hand aide, learning culinary details that made the difference between a meal being just good and out-of-this-world extraordinary.

In the evenings, after the bistro closed, she often sat on the front patio with her easel and paints, duplicating on paper the glow of the moon on the sparkling ocean waters. Below splashes of dark blue and silver-gold, gentle strokes of yellow and brown merged to represent the still-warm sand. Those evenings were magical, filled with the song of crashing waves and the fragrant ocean breeze.

When she sat back to observe her work, she had the eerie sense that the beach sand resembled rolling hills and the moon, big, open skies. Where were those images coming from? She would adjust the easel and look at the painting from different angles in the dim light above the bistro's door, hoping to bring the connection into focus. But she could never figure it out.

Had she traveled as a child and visited a similar landscape? It was unlikely. She was an only child, and she'd lost her parents to a car accident when she was barely three years old. Her grandmother had raised her along the Pacific coast until she herself died just one day after Mist's eighteenth birthday. She was a California girl, for certain. That is, until she arrived in Montana.

Timberton had offered several things she sought – a change of pace, an opportunity to study the landscapes a favorite artist had so beautifully captured and, serendipitously, a way to earn a living. The town was desperate for a decent restaurant, and the ramshackle, vacant eatery had potential. A small room behind the kitchen could serve as a combined studio and living space. It was all she needed.

Turning away from the door, Mist extinguished the café lights and retreated to the back, slipping off her work boots and settling down on a wooden stool. She clipped a fresh sheet of paper on her easel, dipped a slender brush into a mustard-hued paint pot and began.

CHAPTER EIGHT

Paige wrapped her hands around a mug of fresh-brewed coffee and tried to conceal her disappointment. She watched as Jake speared a forkful of raspberry-stuffed French toast, slopped it around in drizzled syrup and popped it into his mouth.

"I don't see why you have to leave so soon," she said, aware she was whining. "You just got here last night."

"I'm not leaving this instant," Jake pointed out. "We have time for a leisurely breakfast." He contemplated a side platter of fresh fruit, neatly cut and artistically displayed. He motioned for Paige to help herself, but she shook her head. He chose a crescent-shaped slice of honeydew melon and added it to his plate.

The morning meal held little of the evening dinner's excitement. Small syrup pitchers replaced the votive candles on the tables, and improvisational jazz replaced Enya. Paige found the jazz especially annoying at the moment. Last night's clear sky and bright moon had evolved into dark clouds instead of sun. The threat of rain was palpable.

Mist appeared beside the table, offering coffee refills. "Java Love?" she asked serenely, holding a thermos-type coffee pot over the table. Even the metal coffee container seemed out of place to Paige.

"Java Love?" Jake asked before Paige had a chance to head off his question.

"Yes," Mist said. "We serve Java Love at Moonglow. It is excellent coffee and beautiful motivation for starting your day."

Paige fought the urge to roll her eyes. Why was she feeling so snippy? She'd been around spoiled preschoolers in her life with better attitudes than her current one. That realization alone made her feel worse.

"I have a large load of lumber being delivered tomorrow at the ranch. I need to be there when it arrives."

Jake's tone was apologetic, though there was no reason for him to be. After all, she hadn't let him know her own plans. If she'd warned him that she was coming, he might have been able to rearrange the delivery.

"Lumber," Paige repeated. Her tone was polite, but cool.

Jake laughed, unable to contain his amusement at Paige's irritation. "Yes, lumber. Dan McElroy's going to help me get the flooring replaced in those cabins on my property. His furniture business has slowed down since the tourist season is over. He can use the work, and I can use help getting as much done as possible before the heavy snow comes, which could be any day now."

"Oh, that reminds me!" Paige snapped out of her pout at the mention of Dan McElroy's name. "I need to get him rent for that little cabin of his I used when I was out here last time. I asked him to hold it when I thought Susan was sending me back to Jackson Hole."

"Don't worry, he's holding it," Jake said. "And don't worry about the rent, either. He's not going to let you pay for time you're not there."

Paige set down her fork. "But that's not right. He could be renting it to someone else."

"He doesn't want to rent it to anyone else," Jake said. "He hadn't rented it for years before you came to Jackson. Seems he had some bad experiences in the past. He'd rather have it empty than have some deadbeat renter in there. He likes the idea that someone he can trust will come back now and then." Jake put down his own fork and took Paige's hand. "And so do I."

* * * *

"How's the research going?" Paige could hear the manic sounds of the newsroom in the background of her conversation with Susan.

Paige could visualize the scene. Susan would be standing over her desk multi-tasking, sorting files and photos, while a fax machine behind her spewed out documents at warp speed. The glaring overhead lighting would make the rushed activity around the editing department seem electric. The aroma of coffee would float through the office, an energy lifeline for the staff. Brandi, undoubtedly, would be hovering around her own desk, refreshing her makeup and tapping the tips of her glittered manicure against her phone, waiting for someone to die. Paige shuddered and said a silent prayer of thanks that she was working "Features" instead of "Obits."

"It's coming along. I need to do more fact-checking, but focusing on the Yogo sapphires seems to be the best way to go."

"Sounds ideal," Susan said. It wasn't always easy to match advertisers with feature articles, but this was a perfect scenario. The story would sell the ads. In turn, the ads would draw attention to the story.

"This will make our advertising department happy. They're already hitting up the local jewelers to buy large display ads. Sold a few already. Revenue forecasts are up for the week of the convention."

Susan's voice faded while she answered a question away from the phone. As always, the office sounded hectic.

"If Brandi's not too busy, maybe she could check around for information on sapphire deposits out here." Backup research could be both helpful and expedient. In spite of her eccentricities, Brandi wasn't bad at rustling up information. "And it'd be good to track down jewelers who already have Yogos in stock."

"I'll get her working on it."

"Thanks, anything might help. Besides, it'll keep her busy between funerals."

"You're not getting sidetracked chasing another story this time, are you?" Susan's tone was both teasing and serious.

Paige winced. Articles that started out as one thing had a tendency to turn into something else when Paige was on the road – sometimes for the better, sometimes not, depending on the paper's needs.

"Of course not," she lied. After all, was it her fault that sapphire mining and western art crossed paths geographically?

"Any close encounters of the cowboy kind?" Now Susan was definitely teasing her. After years working for the paper, Paige knew her work ethic wasn't in question.

"As a matter of fact, I did have one recently," Paige laughed. "So odd that he knew where I was."

"I took a chance with that one, but it was a pretty safe bet that you wouldn't mind."

"You knew I wouldn't." The memory of Jake's visit eclipsed Paige's disappointment over his heading back to Jackson.

Susan called out to someone else in the department, asking if any photos had been delivered. Hearing a "yes," she turned back to the call with Paige. "Gotta go, email me an update." The line disconnected as Paige said goodbye.

CHAPTER NINE

Paige studied the interior of the gem gallery more closely on her second visit. Aside from the business, Clive's place itself was intriguing. Its walls held a variety of encased or framed items. One glass case held a collection of old mining tools – rusted picks and clamps. Unfamiliar as Paige was with mining methods, the objects didn't mean much to her and probably wouldn't add to her article on sapphires. But it was fascinating to see the basic tools that miners had used during early years.

As she wandered along the wall, she passed a framed newspaper article featuring the gem gallery. Dated a few years earlier, it read more like an advertisement than an article. The accompanying photo showed Clive leaning against a post outside the front entrance, a pleased-with-himself smile plastered across his face and the bright, wordy, painted front window to his side.

Paige listened idly to Clive's conversation with some tourists from Omaha who were on their way to Butte to visit relatives. They hoped the side trip to Timberton might allow them to pick up a sparkling trinket or two. It sounded like Clive was well on the way to coaxing them into a third attempt. He succeeded, quickly setting up new piles of gravel and leaving them to their treasure hunt.

When he caught up to Paige to say hello, she was standing in front of a striking painting, a western scene in a thick, gold frame. The framing would not have been her first choice for artwork with an Old West theme. Something more rustic would have worked better. But the painting itself was remarkable and reminded her of others she had seen in museums.

"Nice, isn't it?"

"Yes," Paige agreed, stepping back to get a broader view of the piece. "Is this a Charles Russell painting? I've seen a few of his, and they look a lot like this one."

Clive laughed and shook his head. "No, I wish. I could close the shop and retire in comfort."

"It's a spectacular likeness, in that case," Paige said, tilting her head to the side and studying the piece from another angle.

"Indeed it is," Clive agreed. "And there's a reason for that. A student of his painted it. From what they say, Mr. Russell was never pleased with this particular student, and, it's true, this student's earlier works lacked something. But the later paintings showed huge improvement. Maybe it just took some time and practice for him to get it right. Too bad Mr. Russell was long gone by the time his student's work improved to the point of gaining a local name for himself. Word has it that the teacher-student relationship between them was rocky."

"Really," Paige kept her tone light, hoping she sounded less intrigued than she suddenly was. She tilted her head and took in the overall composition. It was detailed, a vivid scene of horses descending a hill beneath a brilliant blue sky with soft, wispy clouds. The angles of the horses' legs galloping captured their movement beautifully. Clouds of dust sprang up alongside their hooves. Though the horses moved as a herd, the varied coloring of the individual horses made each one stand out on its own. Below, a covered wagon rested in a shaded valley, a glowing campfire alongside it.

It was an impressive painting, rich in western imagery. But even more intriguing to Paige was the way the piece fell in line with descriptions in the old diary. Tempted to bring up the discovery to get Clive's opinion, Paige thought better of it. It would be wiser to figure out the connection herself.

Her eagerness to find the missing entries was growing stronger by the minute. The painting in Clive's gallery was certainly linked to the person who had kept the diary.

Leaning forward, Paige examined the lower right corner of the canvas. "SJW?" The signature was abrupt, the letters close together. With the exception of the additional "J," it matched the printing in the front of the diary.

Clive nodded. "Silas Wheeler, Russell's student."

"His signature is bold." Paige took in the angular formation of the initials. The brush strokes were compact and solid. She resisted an odd urge to reach out and touch the surface.

"Well, he was a bold man." Clive glanced over his shoulder to check on his customers. Finding them absorbed in their sapphire hunt, he turned back to face Paige.

"Not much is known about Silas Wheeler. He lived here in Timberton, but shipped most of his paintings off to be sold in other areas. Silas was a gruff old curmudgeon. All anyone ever got out of him were grumblings and complaints."

"Sounds like a temperamental creative type," Paige suggested, attempting to give the character the benefit of the doubt.

Clive laughed. "You're giving him too much credit. The guy was a downright arrogant jerk who believed his talent gave him the right to be condescending. He kept to himself, which was fine with the townsfolk here, seeing as he had nothing pleasant to say to anyone. He was erratic and unpredictable, prone to sudden bursts of anger. They say he threw a fit one day just because the general store didn't carry a certain product he needed. Picked up a jug of whiskey and sent it flying through the store's front window and then kicked over a barrel of apples for good measure. Walked right out the door, broken glass crunching under his feet. The shopkeeper just cleaned it up and let him go. No one wanted to mess with him."

Paige took another close look at the painting. "He was remarkably talented."

"Yeah, I guess he was, at least in his later years," Clive said. "Don't know why someone talented would be so cantankerous. He had plenty to be grateful for. Maybe he was bitter because it took most of his life to develop his skill. Who knows?"

A squeal of excitement from the worktable sent Clive ambling over to inspect a stone that had been found by one of the customers. As the visitors had hoped, they'd managed to find a small sapphire. Their enthusiasm was dampened when Clive explained the cutting and polishing process would reduce its size. But they left in good spirits, taking an order form with them, in case they decided to have the stone processed later on.

Paige pried herself away from the painting and joined Clive at the worktable.

"Do many people go ahead and have the stones cut?" Paige keyed in on a possible aspect for *The Manhattan Post* article, setting aside the subject of Silas Wheeler and his paintings.

Clive stretched both arms across the table, gathering the leftover gravel into a pile. "No, they don't. Every now and then someone will, but it's rare that a stone will be large enough to be cut into a gem. Doesn't matter, really. They enjoy the process and learn a little bit about the area at the same time."

"And it gives this town some business, as well."

"Yep, that's the idea. And sometimes they'll buy a readymade piece of jewelry with a decent sized stone." Clive grinned like a mischievous schoolboy. The salesman was back.

* * * *

Betty was folding brochures for the hotel when Paige returned from the gem gallery. A vacuum cleaner sat on the edge of the lobby's rug, and a dust rag rested on the edge of the main counter.

"Where's your handsome visitor?" Betty practically glowed. She was clearly proud that she'd pulled off Jake's surprise visit so well.

"He's on his way back to Jackson. He has to be at his ranch for a lumber delivery. Sneaky of you, setting up that dinner at Moonglow the way you did." Paige's involuntary smile canceled the fake scolding tone.

"Well, that's quite a ways to drive for such a short visit. I think that man's mighty sweet on you." Betty placed a few folded brochures in a display rack and started in on another batch. "He's quite a looker, too."

"That he is," Paige sighed.

"Those blue eyes, good manners and that cowboy swagger make me wish I could wind the clock back about four decades. How'd you meet him, you being from way back east?"

"Another work assignment," Paige said. "An article on gold prospecting in Jackson Hole. I'd never been out this far west before that. It was an eye-opener."

"And I've never been as far east as New York. Must be a whole different life out there."

"Yes, it is." Visions of Manhattan flashed through Paige's mind. New York and Timberton were about as similar as the moon to Earth. The tallest structure in Timberton would barely reach the second floor of her office building.

"So how's that slick gem dealer doing," Betty asked, with a mix of curiosity and disdain.

"Clive seems like a nice enough guy. He certainly knows the history of sapphire mining around here, which is exactly what I need."

"He certainly knows the business of luring the tourists in, is more like it." Betty shook her head. "I can't imagine how many people must walk out of there disappointed. Must be a better way to spend money on vacation."

"I don't know," Paige said. "I watched a family sort through a couple of piles of gravel today, and they were pretty excited to find a small stone. They seemed happy when they left."

"That stone won't amount to anything," Betty said. "Cut it down and it'll be the size of a pin head."

"I think it's the experience the tourists are looking for," Paige suggested.

"Ha!" Betty clearly didn't buy it. "Don't fool yourself. They're after a rock the size of Princess Di's."

Paige laughed. "From what I've read, that famous sapphire of Diana's could have come from anywhere."

"I suppose so, not that it matters to me. I'm not much into jewelry," Betty stated. "A waste of good money." Under the grumbling, Paige thought she heard a touch of longing in Betty's voice.

CHAPTER TEN

Paige took an apple from the hotel's front counter and headed upstairs to her room. For no rational reason, she checked the empty wall cavity, as if missing portions of the diary might have materialized while she was away. Of course there was nothing, which set her mind spinning with curiosity. She needed to find a way into lower sections of the wall. Asking Betty to help was one option. Doing so might fill in some of the gaps, provided the hotelkeeper had any idea where the diary came from. But Paige had the current advantage of being the only one who knew of the diary's existence, except for Jake. Better to wait before sharing the discovery locally. Finding the missing portion was more important.

She tried to remember the layout of the lower hallway. What about the room below hers? Exhausted from the plane flight and drive, she'd only looked at rooms on the top floor, settling on the quiet one she currently occupied. Thinking back, she recalled Betty saying the one below hers was used for laundry. She considered going downstairs to check the wall below. But she paused at the sound of Betty's footsteps in the lobby. She would have to wait.

Shedding the jeans and sweatshirt she'd casually thrown on that morning, she lifted a red, flannel nightshirt over her head and let it slip down over her arms and shoulders. She folded down the bedding, sat down and checked her cell phone for messages. Seeing voicemail from New York, she leaned back against the pillows and played the first one, expecting Susan's voice.

Paige? Hey, it's Brandi! We miss you back here in the Big Apple! You're not getting tied up out there with that cowboy are you? Brandi's voice morphed into a laugh as she realized the accidental double entendre. *Sorry! Anyway, I've been going over your article outline and discussing it with the advertising staff...that is, Susan asked me to see what they thought...and they...OH, and I forgot to tell you! Bergdorf's having a sale and I found the most AMAZING purse, Italian leather, dyed the most fab purple you've ever seen, with rhinestones on the handle. Swarovski, no less...But, back to the sapphire article....*This was followed with a scuffling sound and a smack that promised to be the sound of the phone hitting the office floor. *Wait, Susan's waving at me, I'll call you back. Ciao!*

Paige smiled. Brandi could drive both of them crazy. But she meant well and they both knew it.

Moving on to the second message, she was greeted again, as expected, with Brandi's voice.

Paige? Sorry! I dropped the phone and then Susan...well, anyway, I checked into the sapphire deposits out there, like you asked. Read all about Montana. Wow! Sure isn't anything like New York out there, is it? ... Another scuffling sound, this time not a phone hitting the ground, but what Paige guessed was a bag of chips being ripped open. She could only imagine Brandi's scrunched up brow while reading about the West. It was unlikely she'd ever been west of Hoboken. Paige pulled the phone away from her ear quickly as a loud crunch came through the line. *So, I found those big mining areas you emailed about – creek, river, whatever, but also small ones ... crunch ... lots of small ones, including some near you ... crunch ... you're in Timberton, right? Did you know that's not far from Yogo Gulch? Wait, of course you know that. Anyway, it doesn't really matter. There were hundreds of places they started to dig up and filled back in when nothing was found ... crunch ... So you're on the right track with Yogo Gulch. I want one of those Yogos, too, to go with my turquoise yoga pants and lime green floor mat ... Ha! Get it? Yogo? Yoga? ... Oh! And Rachel Rose Bernice Hortzenberg died! I know, I know, we have no idea who she was, but what a name! Ciao!*

Paige exited her voicemail, pulled a pillow over her head, dropped her arm across the bed and let the cell phone slide out of her hand. With the disconcerting image of Brandi's yoga ensemble in her head, she fell asleep.

CHAPTER ELEVEN

Paige bolted upright in bed, dazed in the pitch-dark room. Steady pounding on her door, coupled with the sound of sirens, shocked her awake in seconds. She jumped out of bed and rushed to the door, opening it so quickly that Betty's next knock almost smacked her in the forehead.

"Hurry, Moonglow is on fire!" The hotelkeeper was frantic, and her distress was contagious. Paige pulled on jeans, shoes and a jacket without bothering to take off her nightshirt. She was out the door within seconds behind Betty.

"Is the hotel in danger?" Paige shouted as they rushed toward the sidewalk. Smoke filled her nostrils and throat. She cupped a hand over her face, but the gesture was useless. The air was thick; there was no escaping the black billows flowing from the café. The sheriff's car raced by, siren shrieking, lights flashing against the dense, smoky night sky.

Betty shook her head. "I don't think so. The buildings on each side of Moonglow are much newer, mostly concrete and steel. Unlikely the fire will spread. But Mist's place is in trouble. That building is nothing but wood and is old as the hills." They pushed forward until they reached the perimeter of the fire-engulfed property. Panic was as thick in the air as the smoke.

Two fire trucks were parked at haphazard angles in front of the café, hoses sprouting from them. A crew of men clad in waterproof gear faced the building and aimed blasts of water at the bright flames that flowed from the front windows. The firefighters were determined, but it was clear they were no match for the growing fireball in front of them.

Sheriff Myers' car screeched to an abrupt halt. He jumped out and screamed to the townspeople already congregated to stay back. Rushing forward, he shoved people, including Paige, to the side.

"Is there more help coming?" Paige shouted at him over the commotion.

"I said stand back!" The sheriff growled and stared directly at Paige. "You're in my way, lady!"

"I'm afraid this town only has two fire trucks and crew," Betty said, pulling Paige aside, "one fire chief – Clayton, the guy over there giving orders – and a few volunteers." Betty's eyes brimmed with tears, sparkling in the reflection of the flames.

"What about neighboring towns?"

"Too far away," Betty said. "They'll probably send some help, but by the time it gets here, the damage will be done. This is going up too quickly."

Paige stared at the burning building, feeling paralyzed. The crowd was growing rapidly. Timberton residents shouted across the chaos to each other, asking questions and forming premature theories about the cause of the fire.

"Must've started as a grease fire!" one voice shouted. His suggestion was quickly shot down.

"It's the middle of the night, you idiot. Why would anyone be cooking?" Murmurs from others confirmed that most agreed.

"Electrical, then," a young man's voice chimed in. "Plenty of things not up to code in these old buildings. Isn't this Clive Barnes' building? I bet he hasn't updated anything in years."

"Now wait a second," Betty shouted, angry now. "We can't just go accusing people of things we know nothing about. Just pipe down. There'll be a proper investigation. Right now we need to stay out of the way and not make things worse by speculating." The crowd clearly sided with Betty, and some people chastised those starting rumors.

The conversation snapped Paige out of her temporary numbness. "Where is Clive?" She stepped back and looked around. "And where is …?" A sudden horror gripped her as she faced Betty abruptly and grabbed her by both arms.

"Where's Mist? Doesn't she live in the back of the café?" Paige knew the answer immediately by the terror on Betty's face. Paige let go of Betty, pushed her way through the mob of people and raced toward the sheriff, who stood with his back to the crowd and his arms extended as if he were a human barricade.

Paige pulled on Myers' sleeve to get his attention. "Sheriff Myers! A woman lives in the back of the café, Mist, the one who runs it! Have you seen her? Did the fire chief say anything about her?"

Myers swiveled toward Paige and pushed her back. "Lady, get away from the fire! I don't know nothing about anyone being in that building. Now get back, or I'll arrest you for obstruction."

Paige stepped back and found the man Betty had identified as the fire chief. "Did you check the back room of the café?" She could barely hear herself shout.

Clayton shook his head. "No, the heat was already too intense when we arrived. We're focusing on containment, keeping it from jumping to other structures."

"But the café owner lives in that back room!" Paige screamed. She felt sick. By the look on the fire chief's face, she wasn't alone. He raced off, shouting at another member of his department while Paige did a rapid about-face and rushed back to Betty, who collapsed into her arms as she reached her.

Paige buckled under the hotelkeeper's dead weight, and both hit the ground. Loose gravel dug into Paige's cheek, and a searing pain soared up her arm. The shock of hitting the ground roused Betty. Her eyes fluttering, she struggled to sit up. Paige did the same.

A few of the townsfolk turned from watching the fire and soon hovered above the two women on the ground. When Paige looked up, she could barely make out the shapes of their heads, backlit by fire and smeared from the surrounding smoke. She was grateful when a pair of hands reached down to help Betty up. A wail of thanks escaped Betty's lips. The same strong arms pulled Paige to her feet, where she found Clive standing in front of them both.

"Mist!" Paige stammered, waving her uninjured arm in the direction of the blazing café. Betty broke into sobs and leaned over, resting her hands on her knees.

"What about Mist?" Clive asked. His gaze flickered between the distraught women and his burning building. His face looked dark and strained against the drama of the fiery background.

Paige struck him with both fists to get his full attention. "She's in there! Mist is in the café! We have to get her out!"

Clive bent forward, looked Paige in the eyes and put his hands on her shoulders to help her focus. "Slow down, darlin'. Mist isn't in the café. She's at the gem gallery."

It took a few seconds for the words to sink in. Betty let out another wail, this time of relief.

"She's...she's at your store?" Paige was bewildered.

"Yes, she's fine." Clive said. "Oh! You thought...! Oh, no wonder you two were behaving like crazed hens! Mist called me when she first smelled smoke, and I told her to get out. She ran down to the store while I called the fire department."

Clayton approached Clive, running the back of one forearm across his ash-covered brow.

"I'm sorry, Clive. Not much left we can do." Smudges of soot plastered his face, and muddy water dripped off his fire-resistant jacket.

"You've given it your best shot, Clayton. No one was injured, that's the important thing."

Betty looked like she was about to head for the ground again, so Paige linked her good arm through Betty's to help hold her upright.

Clive glanced at Paige and Betty briefly before he turned to watch his building burn. "You two get back to the hotel. Nothing you can do here."

Paige was mesmerized as she watched the firefighters, who now had control of the flames. What was once a café was now a smoky mess of burnt wood and embers. When she looked at Clive to see how he was holding up, she realized he'd spoken to her. He nodded in the direction of the hotel. "Go on, now," he said.

Reluctantly, Paige left Clive standing in front of the smoldering café. Although Clive's voice was calm and strong, his expression was discouraged and stricken.

As Paige and Betty left the frenzy and heat of the fire scene, they felt the night chill return. By the time they reached the hotel, they were shivering and grateful for the lobby's warmth.

"I'll make some coffee," Betty said, heading for the kitchen. "I'm too keyed up to sleep." If Paige hadn't witnessed it, she never would have believed this energetic, forceful woman had fainted just a few minutes ago.

"That makes two of us," Paige said. "I'll join you." She followed Betty and took a seat at the kitchen's center table. As they were starting into refills, someone knocked on the door. Clive.

"Saw the lights on," Clive said, taking a seat alongside Paige. "You two took a good tumble back there. Thought I'd see how you were."

"I'm fine," Betty said, her back to Clive as she turned to retrieve the coffee pot.

"Just sore and bruised," Paige said, as she rubbed her arm then stretched and bent it to show she was fine. "Nothing compared to what you've suffered."

"Well, I appreciate everyone's sympathy, but the building isn't the only thing we lost tonight. A piece of Timberton's history went up in flames." Clive shook his head as Betty handed him a mug of coffee.

"It was one of the original structures, wasn't it?" Despite her fatigue, Paige had a ream of questions in her mind.

Clive nodded, his face solemn. "You bet it was. Old as the hotel. You know how people say 'if walls could talk'? That building was a perfect example. Been a part of this town just about as long as there's been a town to be a part of."

"Lots of history, then," Paige mused. "What was it before?"

"Oh, it was lots of things over the years." Clive ran a hand from his forehead back through his hair, as if trying to dig up old memories.

"Before Mist came to town, the building was empty. Had been for a while. But there were a few other businesses in that building over the last few decades: an antique store, an appliance repair store, a soda shop. Nothing that lasted very long. Most just stayed a season, then closed up and moved on. There's just not much in Timberton to keep a business going year-round."

Paige's curiosity wasn't about to stop at that. Decades were tidbits of time compared to a century of existence.

"What was the first business in the building, do you remember?"

"No, I don't remember. It was vacant for a long time. When I bought it, it needed repairs badly. Probably why it sat empty for so long. The walls were pretty well built, thank goodness, but the roof might as well have been a showerhead when it rained. Some of the plumbing needed to be replaced, and the front steps had cracked and crumbled. It was boarded up for at least fifteen years before I was able to gather up enough cash to buy it."

"I'm surprised it even withstood that much time, the upkeep ignored as much as it sounds."

Clive nodded. "Well, they built things nice and sturdy way back then. Put in some elbow grease and used good, solid wood. Not like nowadays."

Again, Clive paused, staring down at his coffee. The reality of the calamity continued to sink in.

"It wasn't always neglected," he added. "At least I don't think it was. I know that old coot never kept it up any. But other tenants over the years must have treated it better, or it would've been gone a long time ago. Many of our old buildings are gone, most to fires."

"What old coot?" Paige couldn't stifle her curiosity. And maybe talking would ease Clive's understandable distress.

"Huh?" Clive looked up. "Oh, that artist, the one who painted that piece you like so much at the gallery."

"Silas Wheeler, right? He lived there?" Paige took a sip of coffee, tilted her head to the side and waited for Clive's answer.

"No, he just used it as a studio, gave lessons there now and then. He lived here in the hotel. Like I said when you first saw that painting, he kept to himself, which was just fine with folks around town. He threw fits if things didn't go his way. Probably a good thing he left town not long after I set up shop. If he'd ever thrown one of his tantrums in my place, I would've given him a piece of my mind and probably a tad bit more."

Paige touched Clive's arm gently. "I'm so sorry about your building."

"Well, like I said, no one was hurt." He stood, downed his coffee, set the mug on the table and headed out. "I'd better get back to the gallery and check on Mist."

Paige and Betty cleared the mugs from the table as Clive left.

"Betty, I was just wondering, do you have old registration files for hotel guests?"

"Oh, gosh, yes." Betty's eyes were half-mast with fatigue. "There's a stash of old registers that go way back."

Paige hesitated. It had been a long, stressful night. But she'd never been able to resist following a hunch. "If it's no bother, I'd like to see them. Not now, of course," she said quickly.

"No problem, dear. I'll look for them in the morning."

Paige shooed Betty toward her room and headed up the stairs to her own. Pulling off the jeans and other clothing she'd thrown on in her rush, she paused to glance behind the radiator at the cavity in the wall. Tomorrow promised to be a day of research.

CHAPTER TWELVE

Paige slipped down the stairs the following morning, half-awake and barefoot. She shouldn't have been surprised to find Mist, Clive and half a dozen other townsfolk sitting in the lobby of the hotel. Yet, she was. The café fire had haunted her night like a bad dream, just a dream. But the sight of the gathering in the lobby brought her back to reality. Of course people had come to the hotel. Where else would they go? Moonglow had been the morning meeting place for the entire town. Seeking coffee and consolation, it was natural everyone would turn up at the hotel.

Paige found Betty behind the hotel counter refilling coffee pots as fast as she could. The women exchanged a look that acknowledged last night's disaster. Paige filled a mug with the steaming java, and Betty went back to the kitchen to continue brewing.

The mood in the lobby was somber, like the gathering for a funeral. And, in essence, that's what it was for many of the residents – the realization of a sudden and unexpected goodbye to a part of town life that they had loved.

Mist, the most upset among them, sat near the hotel's main front window. Her eyes, normally serene and peaceful, were glazed and red-rimmed. Her hands, the same ones that had glided plates onto tables as lightly as feathers floating from the sky, grasped each other nervously. Paige placed a light hand on Mist's shoulder.

"Mist, I'm so sorry." What else was there to say?

Clive tried to hand Mist a mug of coffee. She ignored it. Clive nodded, glanced at Paige and took a sip of it himself. Tapping Paige's elbow to lure her out of Mist's earshot, he moved across the room and settled against a wall opposite the front window.

"She's devastated," Clive said.

The hotel door opened quietly, and Paige watched Sheriff Myers slip in. He saw Mist at the window and went to her immediately.

"Miss? I'd like to talk to you about what happened to your café."

Mist looked out the window as if he were not only silent but also invisible. Clive left Paige briefly to speak with Myers.

"I can't get her to talk, either," he said.

"Well, if she starts talking, have her call me," Myers said. He left the townspeople to grieve on their own.

Clive rejoined Paige.

"She's in shock, Clive. I mean, I'm in shock myself, and I didn't just lose my entire business, not to mention ...." Paige paused a second, letting the full picture sink in. "What about her artwork? I didn't even think of that before." A shudder ran down Paige's back. Mist had likely lost both her business and years of work.

"Most of that is at my place," Clive said. "That little back room was barely big enough for a bed, much less storage room for artwork. Good thing, it turns out."

"There were a few pieces on the walls." Paige's memory scanned the lost café's interior.

"Well, those are gone, unfortunately. But it could have been much worse." Clive took another sip of coffee and closed his eyes, resting against the hotel wall.

"Hollister!" A voice broke the lull. Several heads snapped around, searching for the source.

"I said who will feed Hollister?" said Mist.

"What do you mean, who will feed Hollister?" Clive asked.

Mist looked around the now silent room as if its occupants spoke another language. It was so clear to her. The homeless needed food, just like anyone else.

"I always put a plate out for him, every morning and every night. On the back steps because I can't get him to come inside." She turned back to the window.

"Heck, forget that old guy. Who'll feed me?" The comment came from the same young man who'd spit out rash theories about the fire the night before. A couple of his buddies snorted with laughter.

"Tommy, shut the hell up," Clive barked. "Where's your compassion? This isn't about you. This young woman just lost her livelihood. And I lost a building, and the town lost a piece of history. There's a lot of heartbreak going on here and your breakfast ain't a part of it."

Murmurs of agreement circled the room, including many from those who'd wondered the same thing about breakfast but had held their tongues. Common decency made it clear that a couple of slices of toast at home would be on the menu this particular morning.

"I'll take him some coffee," Betty said, sharing a sudden communal shame. Had it never occurred to anyone to wonder how Hollister was getting food? She poured a mug from the freshest pot and headed for the front door.

"He won't be out there yet." Mist's voice was little more than a whisper. "Not this early."

Betty paused at the front door.

"He'll be down by the trestle, at least until it warms up later this morning." The townsfolk suddenly realized that Mist had been taking care of all of them, not just those who frequented Moonglow.

"It's no warmer under that trestle than it is in the square, stupid fool." More snorts and laughter.

"Tommy, I'm warning you, this is your last chance to zip yer lip, or I'll throw you out of here myself." Clive glowered at Tommy. The young punk and his sidekicks laughed off Clive's threats but left on their own.

The room's focus was back on Mist, who continued to stare out the front window. Clive rubbed his chin then spoke.

"Mist, I hate to agree with that young jerk, but it's no warmer under that trestle than anywhere else outside. Why would he be there?"

The muscles in Mist's face relaxed into something resembling a smile despite her sadness. "Because he's not outside."

"Not outside? I don't understand." Confused discussion circled the room, one theory following another. It was Clive who came up with the closest guess.

"You're not talking about that old grate in the concrete, are you?" Clive scratched his head. "That thing's been rusted shut for decades. It was some sort of drainage pipe, I think."

The room erupted with the sound of confused voices.

"How can it be a drainage pipe? It's not on the ground; it's on the wall."

"Yeah, that grate is under the trestle, but up against the south side."

"Nothing can drain into a wall. That's ridiculous."

Comments came from all directions.

"It is not a drainage pipe," Mist explained. "It never was. It just looks like one." She took a deep breath, exhaling slowly. "It is actually a passageway."

"A passageway!" Surprised chattering made the rounds of the room. Clive looked more confused than anyone. "A passageway to where? "

Exhausted, Mist sighed. "It does not lead anywhere. It ends about twelve feet in, widening at the end, like a small room. The space keeps him out of the wind. He has blankets. Sometimes I take him food from the café. That is, I used to." Mist's eyes filled with tears.

"What?" Clive rubbed his chin again, a sign of hard thinking, Paige decided. "I don't know anything about a passageway or room under that trestle, and I've lived in Timberton all my life. You sure you're not imagining some metaphysical room or something, Mist?"

"Too much herbal tea and maybe a few of those California brownies, if you know what I mean," a bystander whispered.

Tires crunching on gravel outside caused the conversation to pause. A sharp metal slap signaled the slamming of the vehicle's door, and, a few seconds later, the oldest, gruffest cowboy Paige had ever seen walked into the hotel. Dust covered every inch of the man, from his scuffed hat down to his weatherworn boots. Scruffy eyebrows and a matching beard added to his bizarre appearance.

"Well, now," Clive exclaimed. "If it isn't William Guthrie himself!" A few murmurs floated around the room.

"Better known as 'Wild Bill' around here," Betty whispered to Paige.

"What brings you up into town today?" Clive asked.

The old cowboy aimed a thumb over his shoulder in the direction of his truck. "I heard about the fire. Mighty sorry about it, ma'am." He turned toward Mist and tipped his hat. "And I was thinkin' you all might need some breakfast. So I loaded up what stock I had of eggs and bacon and biscuit-makings and headed on out here."

Betty stepped forward and held up a hand. "You're not planning on cooking, are you Bill?"

Laughter rippled through the crowd.

"No, ma'am, I know better than that," Wild Bill nodded, acknowledging the good-natured jab.

"Well, in that case, bring the supplies on in, and turn them over to the experts," Clive said. He pointed toward the kitchen and grinned slightly at Betty. "I'll help you bring the supplies in, Bill. Anyone else want to lend a hand?" A few hungry and willing volunteers joined them.

Mist stood up and turned away from the front window toward the kitchen. Paige and some of the other townsfolk stopped her before she even took a step.

"You're not working today," Paige said. "We won't let you. You need to allow us to take care of *you*." Half relieved and half reluctant, Mist sank back down in her chair, clearly exhausted. She resumed her silent watch out the front window.

Paige went to the kitchen to offer help, ducking to avoid a case of eggs balanced on Clive's shoulder. Wild Bill set a sack of biscuit mix on the center table, and Betty pulled pans and dishes out of cupboards, stacked the dishes to the side and arranged the pans on top of the stove. As soon as the provisions had all been placed on the table, the men disappeared.

"All for the better," Betty said. "They'd just be in the way. Kitchen's not that big, anyway. Those egos of Clive and Bill alone are enough to fill this whole room."

Pulling up a stool, Paige sat down and scanned for directions on the back of the biscuit mix sack.

"Don't worry about directions," Betty laughed. "Bill's place is a galaxy away from Moonglow, no pun intended. Just throw some water into the mix and when the dough feels sticky, spoon it onto the baking sheets. Won't be fancy, but it'll fill people up."

As Betty dropped strips of bacon into the heated frying pans, the sound of sizzling meat filled the kitchen. All four burners were fired up, each with some sort of cooking pan hovering above the flames. Betty had relegated two of them for bacon, the other two for frying eggs.

Paige filled a pitcher with tap water and poured small portions into a bowl of biscuit mix, pausing repeatedly to check the consistency. Pour, stir, check, pour again, stir, check again. Eventually, it felt moist enough to hold together, yet dry enough to not run all over.

"You'll want to grease those pans first."

Mist had, as was her habit, appeared suddenly in the kitchen without either Paige or Betty noticing her approach. Paige wondered how the girl managed to simply materialize the way she did. Paige could barely walk across a carpeted floor barefoot without sounding like an elephant. Mist glided soundlessly across any surface, the hotel's kitchen linoleum included, even in work boots.

"She's right," Betty said, pausing between bacon flipping to grab a stick of butter from the fridge.

"Hold on, now!" Bill's gruff voice interrupted as he stepped into the kitchen and snatched the butter from Betty's hand. "Why waste this good butter when you've got all that bacon grease? That grease is enough to keep those biscuits from sticking to the pans."

Betty laughed. "Yes, Bill, you're right. And that's also why no one goes to eat at your place. They don't want to risk a coronary." Even Mist smiled. She took the stick of butter from Bill, who threw up his hands in defeat and returned to the front room.

"You don't have to help," Betty reassured Mist. "You've had a terrible shock, and I'm sure we can manage at least a step up from what Bill dishes out."

Mist's voice was serene. "I want to help because helping is calming. Community is calming." She gently unwrapped the butter halfway and ran it across the surface of the pans. Paige spooned soon-to-be biscuits in mounds on top of the slick, buttery surfaces. Mist slid the trays into the oven.

Now that the frenzy of starting breakfast for the crowd in the lobby had passed, Paige's curiosity reclaimed her. She made sure she and the other two women were alone in the kitchen before she spoke.

"Mist, I've been wondering...you said something about a passageway under the Timberton Trestle before. Were you serious? I mean...it would make sense if last night left you a little mixed up. I doubt you slept much."

As always, Mist's answer was smooth and unfettered with extra words. "I know what is around me, below me, above me." It was as simple as that to her. Paige only wished her own, overactive mind could boil life down to such simplicity. She'd been told often that she put too much energy into analyzing everything. Sometimes an answer was just an answer, nothing more. But it wasn't the way her brain was wired. She couldn't help but admire Mist's calm way of living.

"OK, so there's a passage and compartment under the trestle. And you take Hollister's food there if he doesn't pick it up outside the café," Paige repeated, still unconvinced. She winced as she heard the words come out of her mouth. The café no longer existed beyond its ashen remains. "Have you been inside the compartment?" Again she cringed, hoping she didn't sound as skeptical as she felt.

Mist sighed and remained silent for a moment. Paige figured it was probably the closest the girl ever came to being frustrated.

"It's not necessary to see everything to know it's there. It's not necessary for everything to have a reason. Sometimes things just are." Mist paused. "Things just are," she repeated, as if to finalize her point.

Paige moved to the kitchen sink, rinsing her hands under warm water. To her right, a pile of cooked bacon strips rested between layers of paper towels to soak up extra grease.

Betty placed a pan upside down on top of the bacon to keep it warm, checked the progress of the biscuits in the oven and began cracking eggs into pans. Paige was about to drop the subject of the passageway when Mist spoke again.

"For those of you who need to see in order to believe, there are also blueprints." Mist's voice was as hypnotic as always, which made the logical statement seem somehow incongruous.

"Blueprints?" Now Paige was hooked. Evidence was her drug of choice when it came to reporting. That and gossip, which always left a tantalizing trail.

"Not exactly blueprints," Mist clarified. "Drawings, sketches. Some might call it doodling. But it is clear to me. It matches what I feel around me."

Ah, here we go again, Paige thought to herself. Did everything with Mist have to be such a mystery?

"Food ready yet?" This time it was Clive scuffling into the kitchen. Betty flipped an egg and glowered at him.

"Five minutes. Now out of the kitchen." Clive backed away as instructed, though Paige could swear she saw him wink at Betty.

Paige could hear him bellow from the front room as soon as he was back there.

"Don't mess with the folks in the kitchen. It's serious business in there." The cooks heard a round of mostly manly laughter. Betty huffed and began to shovel food onto plates stacked on the counter. "Nothing but trouble, that one," she said.

"Betty, I'm sure he winked at you," Paige teased. Betty huffed again, but the corner of her mouth twitched upward. Paige pulled the biscuits, now a light golden color, from the oven and placed one on each plate.

"One won't do it for those hungry guys." Betty put a second biscuit on each plate. "Oh," she added, turning to Paige. "I found those old hotel registers you asked about. They're in containers on the floor of the hallway closet. Musty and dusty, but you're welcome to take a look."

When Mist carried plates out to the lobby, the crowd cheered. Paige took a single biscuit and headed for the hallway.

* * * *

Three large tubs covered the floor of the hallway closet. Paige sneezed as she moved dusty rags and cleaning supplies aside and dragged the first container into the hall. Prying the lid off, she pulled out one of half a dozen hotel registers and sat down, setting the book in her lap.

Heavy and solid, the bound volume carried the weight of untold stories. How many hundreds of guests had passed through over the years? Each visitor had arrived and departed with a unique story, leaving a signature behind. What had brought the guests to Timberton over the decades? A family vacation? A business trip? An unexpected car problem that forced a stay over? A research project?

Or a place to stay while tutoring a young art student?

Paige opened the register and scanned the first page. Dated 2009, it was far too recent to interest her. Turning to the back cover, she noted the signatures spanned three years, making it the most recent volume, aside from the current register in the hotel lobby. She set it aside and removed the next register from the tub, which covered the preceding two years. The next covered roughly three additional years. One by one, the registers moved backward, partial decades at a time.

Noting the chronological order, Paige set the first registers back in the tub and replaced the lid. She reached for the next tub, her hand hovering while she estimated the years it would contain – two to three years per register, ten to twelve registers per tub. Bypassing the second batch of registers, she moved on to the third. She tossed the lid aside and searched book by book until she came to a register dated 1954 on the first page and 1957 on the last.

The old diary entries had started in the 1920's, but Paige knew Silas could have come to Timberton at any time, bringing the diary with him. Halfway through the book she held, she found what she was looking for – an entry with Silas Wheeler's name, registering him as a hotel guest on February 25, 1955. His signature matched the handwriting that placed the initials in the diary's front cover. Even better, it confirmed what she'd suspected: he had stayed in Room 16, the same one she occupied now.

CHAPTER THIRTEEN

Clive was sweeping the floor of the gem gallery when Paige stepped inside, and he didn't hear her enter. Afraid to startle him, Paige stalled before saying hello. Sensing the presence of another caused Clive to break his concentration and look up.

"I stopped by to ask how you're doing," Paige said. The well-intentioned gesture was unnecessary. Clive's face revealed his frustration. He was not taking the loss of his building well.

"Not sure I feel too much like entertaining." He returned to pushing clusters of dust and small pebbles into piles for discard. He had too much on his mind to put energy into being social.

"You don't have to entertain me, but maybe talking would help? The café building was insured, right?"

Clive leaned the broom against the gallery wall, stuck both hands in his pockets and sighed.

"If it wasn't maybe the town can pull together and hold a fundraiser or something," Paige suggested.

"I've kept it insured. But it won't cover the entire cost to rebuild. Or replace the sweat equity I've poured into it over the years. And then, there's the history. Those things can't be replaced, with or without money. Buildings aren't the same once they're rebuilt. I've seen so many go down in flames over the years. Sometimes it's hard to believe any of the originals are still standing."

"So, will you rebuild?"

"Oh, sure. But not right away. Snow's gonna get heavy soon. Building will have to wait until spring. Gives me time to get the insurance and additional costs straightened out." Clive's discussion of practical plans couldn't mask his depression.

"So, how *about* having a fund-raiser, then?" Paige was always up for a challenge.

A small smile eased Clive's solemn expression. "Young lady, there aren't enough people around this town right now to raise ten bucks." He paused, watching Paige, as if to gauge what else to say. "Besides, I think I've got a plan."

Paige jumped to guess. "Your jewelry? Your designs are original; I'm sure they'd sell if they got out to the right markets."

Clive shrugged his shoulders. "Maybe. I know one of the jewelers back east said he'd be interested in buying some. Real talkative guy – blah, blah, blah. Seemed less interested when I said I used to have a lot more. I had a big stash of loose stones stolen decades ago." He paused rubbed his chin. "That was a mistake, telling him that," he said. "Never tell someone what you don't have. Just tell 'em what you have. Anyway, I wasn't talking about selling my jewelry."

"OK, what's your plan, then?" Paige noted the empty gallery as well as the quiet streets outside. Clive's business was hardly busy enough to pay bills, much less to finance the reconstruction of the café, she guessed.

"I'm thinking about selling that painting, the one you noticed the other day."

"Seriously? Wouldn't you hate to part with it?" Paige turned to look at the piece hanging on the gallery wall.

Clive shook his head. "Not really. It doesn't have any sentimental value. I mean, it's a nice painting, and I like the way it represents the area. But someone who collects art might appreciate it more, and I'd rather have the funds to put toward the café."

Paige crossed the room and stood in front of the artwork, leaning forward to take a closer look. "What do you think the piece is worth?" Her knowledge of the art world was severely lacking, but she hoped Clive wouldn't fall prey to a dishonest buyer. Some con artist might be tempted to take advantage of a down-to-earth guy in need of money.

"I haven't the foggiest idea." Clive's answer was exactly what Paige feared. It was all the more reason to step in and help out.

"Someone at my office is sure to know an art appraiser who can give you an honest answer," Paige offered. "I'll see if anyone recognizes the name Silas Wheeler."

"Old Silas, meanest son-of-a-Winchester to ever wield a Western paintbrush." Clive had resumed sweeping the gallery floor and was now leaning down, pushing the broom under the worktable and dragging it back repeatedly. A few loose pebbles rolled toward him with each sweep.

"We could email a photo and get a rough estimate. Otherwise we'll need to ship it back east." Paige knew Clive might be hesitant to send the piece across the country. The look he gave her confirmed that.

"We'll try a photo first," Paige said. "Maybe there's a history of Silas Wheeler's later paintings being worth more than his early pieces. You've said they improved a lot. An expert might know more about that."

Paige pulled her cell phone out of her pocket and snapped a quick shot. She could do a basic photo edit on her laptop later and send it to the office. Maybe this would give

Brandi something more challenging to do than write up obits or inspect her nails.

"No hurry. Like I said, I'm not planning to get started on rebuilding for a while." Clive's muffled voice floated up from behind the worktable. "Besides, you have your own work to do. How's that article coming along?"

Paige sighed. "Not much progress on it recently. I don't tend to do my best work while buildings are burning down." Paige bit her lip. It wasn't the most sensitive thing to say. "I mean, I've been so concerned about everyone. A story about sapphires seems trivial. But I hope to make some headway tonight. I have everything I need for an outline, thanks to the history of Yogos you gave me the other day."

"Well, I hope you have a gift for blocking out distraction," Clive laughed. "I hear Betty's planning to cook up a big kettle of stew and another hefty batch of biscuits. I think you'll see a lot of townsfolk stopping by the hotel in search of a meal."

"You're probably right." Paige had to agree. She hadn't thought about it, but there weren't any other options, unless people wanted to eat in their own homes or head down to Wild Bill's. And, aside from the fact they were used to being spoiled by Mist's cooking, the drama of the café burning had provided fodder for everything from gossip and speculation to the sentimental sharing of memories. The hotel was likely to be a central gathering place for a while.

"Now that you've pointed that out, I'd better get back there and see what I can get done before the ruckus starts up." She waved at Clive and left the gallery for the hotel.

Thankfully, the lobby was empty, though she could hear Betty humming in the kitchen. Confident that she'd nabbed some uninterrupted time for herself, she hurried up the stairs and settled into her room. Her yearning to continue searching for the rest of the old diary was fierce, especially after her conversation with Clive about the painter, Silas, but she forced herself to concentrate on the assignment. She sat down at the writing table and looked over her notes.

Clive had done a decent job of explaining sapphire mining to her on her first visit to the gallery. But sticking to the basics would only make for yawn-worthy reading. She needed an angle that would tie in with the international aspect of the upcoming New York conference – perhaps the rumored use of Montana sapphires by the English in the crown jewels or Princess Diana's ring, something that would show the United States played a little-known role in the international gem scene. Or was that necessary? Maybe the fact that Yogo sapphires were only mined in that particular Montana area was the real story. They didn't need to compete with sapphires from Sri Lanka, Ceylon and other gem-producing countries. They were unique to Montana. Not only would that be of interest to regular readers and those attending the conference, but it could draw ads in from jewelers, especially those with Yogos in stock.

Switching gears, Paige narrowed down her focus to the mining of Yogo sapphires. This eliminated the need to research Montana's other mining areas and sidestepped the tedious task of comparing Yogos to stones from different areas of the world. There was no reason to get too technical. She would use the rumored tie-in with British royalty as a hook, then move into sapphire mining in Montana, specifically. She'd wrap it up with another quick British reference. It would work.

A plan formed, she pulled a yellow marker out of her bag and started to highlight details specific to Yogos in her notes. She would call Susan in the morning and run the idea by her. In turn, Susan could set the ad department to work soliciting ads from jewelers whose inventory included items with Montana Yogo stones.

Paige sighed. Now she was thinking more like a businessperson than a journalist. She preferred to take a more objective, scholarly approach to reporting, but the potential for advertising dollars would appeal to Susan, no doubt. She could already feel her editor patting her on the back.

CHAPTER FOURTEEN

When Paige returned for yet another visit to the gem gallery, she found Clive hunkered down over a stack of bills and insurance forms at a desk toward the rear of the store.

"Clive, is this the only painting by Silas Wheeler that you have?" Paige asked.

He was concentrating so deeply she had to repeat her question twice before he looked up.

"No, I mean, yes." Clive slid a black pair of reading glasses down his nose and peered over them at Paige's confused expression. "It's the only Wheeler painting I have now, but I had more at one time. Well, they weren't mine. Silas let me sell a few others for him on consignment. They didn't bring in enough to please his ornery self, so he took the last ones back. Pretty much told me where to go."

"Yet he let you keep one," Paige pointed out.

"Hardly," Clive said with a snort. "I found this one in the basement of the café when I was fixing the place up for Mist." He removed his glasses, set them on the desktop and rubbed his eyes. "There was a whole stash of junk down in that basement – easels, brushes, torn up sketches –along with odds and ends from other tenants that rented the building in-between. Seems people used that basement as a catchall. Or a toss-all and never look back, is more like it."

"Were there other paintings in there when you cleaned the basement out?"

Clive shook his head. "No, that was it. If he had others, he must have taken them with him. Who knows where they'd be now. Silas is long gone. Moved up somewhere around Kalispell when he left Timberton some thirty or thirty-five years ago. Heard he hit the bottle pretty hard and died when his liver gave out sometime in the '80s."

"He must have been a terribly unhappy man," Paige said. The anger in the diary entries matched Clive's description of Silas. More and more, Paige was convinced its author and the painter were the same person.

"Well, I don't know about any of that psychology stuff," Clive said. "But he was sure good at making other people unhappy, that much is certain. I never knew anyone who liked him. Certainly none of the old-timers around here did, back when they were alive and kicking. They're all six feet under now."

"So, who bought the paintings that sold?"

"Tourists picked them up when passing through town, the few that sold before Silas took the rest back. They'd come in looking for a Yogo sapphire, and when they didn't find one, they'd leave with a painting, instead – the ones who were willing to put the money out, that is. Silas always wanted too much for them. Just couldn't get it through his head that he wasn't the artist that Russell had been. Bitter man, that Silas."

Paige looked toward the jewelry case at the front of the gallery. "I imagine you did better selling the jewelry, anyway. After all, people come in here looking for gems, not artwork." She walked over to the case and looked at the assortment.

Clive nodded. "That's exactly why I built up that collection. Even if a visitor finds a small stone while sifting through the gravel, it can be tempting to buy something larger. Still, I haven't sold as many pieces as I'd like. This past summer was disappointing. You know, the economy and all that. I built up a pretty good stash, too, not just what you see out here. Could've been sitting pretty if we'd just had more people passing through. Don't go blabbing that around, mind you."

There were very few pieces in the case to begin with, and she doubted he had more than a half dozen others. They'd be locked in his back safe, anyway. "Your secret's safe with me. Doesn't seem like a high-crime town, anyway. I'll bet your crime rate is almost nothing."

"You're right," Clive said. "We're proud of that, too. That time back when my gems were stolen was pretty shocking to the whole town. It's a small community, and we watch out for each other."

Paige nodded, not even tempted to explain how exponentially different the situation was from that in New York City.

"And you've got Sheriff Myers around, so that's probably enough to dampen someone's enthusiasm if temptation strikes. He seems to be everywhere."

Clive laughed. "Yeah, big ego, big badge. He's new, just started a week ago. Won't be here long, I guarantee it. Every now and then the county sends someone down. Give the guy a month or two, and he'll be transferring out. The fire was a fluke, but once that investigation is over, he won't have much to do. A few months later they'll send down a new guy. It'll be the same thing. At least they don't come down too often, so we don't feel like we have someone breathing down our necks all the time."

Paige smiled. "Well, guess it came in handy to have him here when the café burned down. At least he could help keep people back. Gave the firefighters more elbow room."

Bending forward, she took a closer look at a particular pendant that had caught her attention.

"That's true," Clive agreed. "Good timing there. By the way, not to change the subject, but...." Clive slipped a smooth hand under the latch to the display case and opened it.

Clive adjusted his stance and stood tall. Paige was amused and impressed. Only a master salesman could slide a discussion about a sheriff straight into a demonstration of shimmering jewelry in ten seconds flat.

Paige leaned over the open case to look at the jewelry more closely.

"This pin is beautiful. Is that the Timberton Hotel?"

"Yes, it is," Clive said, "with Yogos above it to represent a night sky. That's a special piece, one of a kind and not for sale." He pointed out another piece.

"I designed this one, too," he said, lifting out a pendant. He dangled it in front of her. A ray of sunlight hit it at an angle, sending prisms of blue and gold outward from the piece. Not only was the sapphire breathtaking, but the intricate setting around it was unlike any design Paige had ever seen.

"I wanted to tie the beauty of the Yogo in with the natural surroundings of the area. At the bottom, you have rolling hills. Above that, the moon rises above a landscape of sagebrush and trees."

"A single Yogo," Paige murmured, "a blue moon, rising above the Montana landscape."

"Exactly!" Clive said.

Paige felt spellbound, but managed to pry herself away. She had an assignment to get back to. Clive picked up on the unspoken shift in subjects and set the pendant back in the case.

"Maybe another day," Clive winked. "Can't blame a businessman for trying, right?"

Paige laughed. "Right," she called on her way out.

CHAPTER FIFTEEN

"I've given Mist a room downstairs," Betty said. "I can use help in the kitchen, what with all these folks looking for food. And she seems lost without the café."

Paige had returned from the gem gallery to find Betty arranging calla lilies and baby eucalyptus for the front lobby. She was relieved to hear the hotelkeeper would have extra help.

"Cooking is art to her." Paige had watched Mist the few times she'd prepared meals since the fire, hands moving gracefully, almost reverently, as she arranged food on plates. "She channels her creativity into cooking the way she channels it into her paintings. It's as if food is her paint; the plate her canvas."

Betty laughed. "I heard Bill exclaim the other day that he didn't know how to eat anything she placed in front of him. Said it was too perfect a picture, and it was easier to chow down food that was just slapped on a plate."

"Like he serves it, I take it." Paige had managed to avoid Wild Bill's since arriving in Timberton.

"Exactly right." Betty acted out her impression of Bill tossing food haphazardly on a plate, holding the imaginary dish out to Paige. Holding up two hands, Paige played along, refusing the food, then pulled a stool up to the center table and leaned forward, placing her elbows on the counter.

"Clive's talking about selling that painting he has hanging on the wall in the gem gallery, hoping it'll bring in a little money to help rebuild the café."

"Ha!" Betty's eyebrows rose. "That old thing he found in the basement when he was cleaning out the café for Mist? He won't get much for it."

"It was painted by a local artist, the way I hear it. Maybe it's valuable," Paige said, ever optimistic.

"Don't count on it," Betty said. "If Clive wants to raise money with painting, he oughta throw some paint on the front of that ugly building of his. Might bring some customers in, rather than scaring them away before they even step foot inside." Betty's lips pressed firmly together. Paige could have sworn the hotelkeeper's posture stiffened up.

"Have you and Clive always jousted like this?" Paige couldn't help asking. It was clear this was a running routine between them.

"No, not always," Betty said, her expression guarded. "There was a time…." Her words trailed off. Paige tried to keep herself from prying but, as often was the case, failed.

"A time when things were different ….?" Paige verbally nudged Betty for more information.

"It was a long time ago." Betty clipped the last of the greenery with a sharp snip, tossed the cutting shears back in the drawer and slammed it shut, ending the discussion.

CHAPTER SIXTEEN

Betty sat down in the tapestry-covered chair alongside the windowsill of her room. A chilly stream of air brushed across her face. She reached out with a flat palm and held it over a crack in the window's weather stripping. Sure enough, it was the source of the inward leak. She'd need to have it sealed or the heating bills for the hotel would show the damage. They were high enough as it was. Each month it became more of a challenge to pay the bills. Even activity at the height of the recent tourist season had fallen short of previous years. She'd heard people say the economy was improving, but her bank account said otherwise.

It was everything she could do to keep the inside of the hotel inviting. The exterior had long ago fallen into disrepair, and the landscaping retained none of its past charm. It was too much for one person, even with Mist's help – handling the reservations, keeping up the rooms and arranging special events for guests.

Even more daunting was coordinating needed repairs, some planned and some popping up without warning at the most inopportune times – for example, just before guests arrived. Occasionally, just in the nick of time, a problem would seem to fix itself. This didn't fool Betty. It was a small town, and people watched out for each other, not always taking credit for impromptu good deeds. There was a good chance Clayton and his crew were sneaking in a few repairs when she wasn't looking. And she wouldn't put it past Mr. Hodges to play handyman once a week, even with his bad hip. But it was still a struggle to keep the hotel running smoothly.

For a long time, Clive had been telling her it wasn't realistic for a woman to run a business that size by herself. Some days she secretly agreed with him, but there wasn't a chance in tarnation she was going to give him the satisfaction of admitting it. Why should she? He'd had no problem with a woman running the place when Abby was still alive. Sweet Abigail, everyone's favorite. It's just how it was. Abby had been the social sweetheart of the town. Older by two years, Abby was always the more extraverted of the two sisters. Prettier, too, though no one said so aloud, of course. But it was obvious from the way men always flocked around her. And Clive had been right there in line with the rest of them. Probably would've asked Abby to marry him if she'd been around longer.

Betty had been the sister who stood in the shadows. A little plainer, a little plumper, she was always the one reading a good book in the corner chair. Or she was out in the garden, planting a rainbow of annuals each spring. When Abby's battle with cancer began to drain her strength, Betty stepped in and started picking up chores around the hotel. In time, Abby was gone, and Betty was left on her own with the hotel.

That was a good twenty years ago, and the town had changed in so many ways. Tourists had come and gone, and she'd always managed to make ends meet. But time had taken its toll on the property, and the list of needed repairs was ever growing. Although Betty's pride had always prevented her from hiring help, now the money just wasn't there. And there was no older sister to step in and lend a hand.

Now she would have help. Others might assume she was bringing Mist on board to help the girl recover from the loss of the café. But Betty knew that she needed the help as much as Mist did.

CHAPTER SEVENTEEN

"Clive is talking about selling a painting he has in order to help rebuild the café."

Paige leaned forward over the writing desk in her room, splitting her attention between the cell phone pressed to her ear and the scribbled notes in front of her. She needed the article outlined before she called the office in the morning.

"Sounds like a decent idea," Jake said.

Paige could hear papers shuffling. Jake was multitasking, as well. The ranch cabins were getting a slow start, considering he'd purchased the property a year before. With winter on the horizon, most of the supplies coming in would need to be stored in the barn until spring.

"I'm worried he doesn't know what he's doing." Paige tapped her pen against the desk's surface as if she could focus Jake's divided attention better. "He has no idea how much it's worth. Silas Wheeler, a student of Charles Russell, painted it. Wouldn't that make it valuable?"

"Maybe yes, maybe no. Has a nice ring to it, unless Wheeler was a lousy painter, in which case it might be worthless."

"True. And that was Russell's opinion." Paige agreed. "Which reminds me, I checked the old hotel registers. Silas Wheeler stayed in this room when he was living here. I'm almost positive that diary I found is his, and his staying here explains why the diary was hidden in this wall."

"Maybe you were meant to find that diary and this story after all since it got you interested in that painting," Jake said. "Clive should have the piece appraised before he sells it," Jake said. "There's no other way to know if it's worth anything."

"That's what I told him," Paige said. "But he seems reluctant to let me send it all the way back to New York. I snapped a photo, but it won't be enough."

"If he's at all willing to have it checked out, he wouldn't have to send it that far. I can send it up to an appraiser in Cody who specializes in western art."

"They have art appraisers in Cody?" Paige laughed, but bit her lip as soon as the words spilled out. Big city snobbery was not attractive.

"Yes, they do," Jake said matter-of-factly. "You'd be surprised at the culture you'd find out here. Your visit to Jackson should have taught you that the Old West is more than a string of saloons and ranches."

"I'm sorry," Paige said. "Of course you're right." She felt herself sink lower in her chair.

"I'm teasing you, Paige. We've got an excellent museum complex in Cody – The Buffalo Bill Historical Center. Five museums right there." Jake paused. Paige could hear him ruffling through paperwork.

"Anyway, I know someone who works in their research center...."

"They have a research center?" Paige sat up a little straighter.

"Yes, believe it or not." Jake paused again. "The McCracken Research Library, home to archived photographs, manuscripts, family papers and rare books about the West."

"And you know someone who works there?"

"Sure do. Doc Lambert. Not the kind of doctor who fixes broken arms, but the kind who spent crazy amounts of time in universities. I'll call him tomorrow and see if he's around. Maybe he can take a look at that painting. You'll have to send it out to him."

"I'll talk to Clive about that." Paige hoped Clive would be willing to send it to Cody. Without an appraisal, he ran the risk of selling it for too low a price. That is, if the painting had any value at all.

"See if Clive wants to have it appraised, and I'll see if Lambert is available. Can't hurt to ask. And I have a hunch you're just going to worry if you don't get some sort of official opinion."

Paige smiled. Jake knew her at least well enough to know she wouldn't let it drop. She was already too attached to the people of Timberton.

The rustling of paperwork on Jake's part paused. His tone softened. "It would be nice to see you again while you're out here."

"It would be nice to see you, too." The sudden shift in conversation surprised Paige, but she didn't mind the change in direction. The idea of seeing Jake again sent a fluttering sensation through her.

"How soon will you be going back to New York?"

Paige mentally ran through her calendar. She really should be able to wrap up the gem article soon if she focused. But the unanswered questions in Timberton begged for more time. There was a chance she could add a few extra Montana days in before heading back east.

"I'm not sure, but I may be able to talk Susan into a few days off after I finish this piece. I'd like to help Betty and Mist sort things out at the hotel. And I like your idea of getting Clive to have the painting appraised. If I linger, I might be able to nudge him into doing it."

Jake laughed. "Paige, if anyone can nudge anyone into anything, it's you. Your middle name is probably Persistence." A pause followed. "What is your middle name, anyway?"

"Kathleen." Paige had always loved her middle name, which she owed to her great-grandmother, Kathleen MacKenzie. A feisty ancestor by reputation, Paige had always suspected she'd inherited some of those traits along with the name. At least, she liked to think so.

"Paige Kathleen MacKenzie." Jake tumbled the words around a few times. "I like the way that sounds. Very dignified, sort of like royalty. Like someone famous."

"Very funny." Paige wasn't sure if Jake was teasing her again or not, but that uncertainty evaporated when a sudden commotion exploded downstairs: shrieks of panic and the sounds of metal crashing.

"I have to go; there's some kind of emergency," Paige said, ending the conversation abruptly. She dropped the cell phone on the bed and raced downstairs where she found Betty frantically attempting to retrieve half a dozen pots and pans from the kitchen floor.

"What happened?" Scooping up a frying pan that almost tripped her as she entered the room, Paige looked around at the scattered cookware.

"My clumsiness, that's what happened." Betty leaned back against the sink counter, out of breath. "I lost my balance hanging a pot on a hook and it fell. That started the dominoes going." A weary swing of her arm indicated a disarray of pots and pans. Paige picked up a saucepan and set it on the center island.

"You look exhausted, Betty, no offense. Isn't Mist helping you today?"

Betty shook her head. "Not this afternoon. She took Hollister a thermos of tea – ginger peach with a touch of honey, I think she said – and then was going to Clive's place. They're trying to figure out a plan of action for the café. It's hard to read that girl, but she seemed discouraged."

"Well, that's understandable. I'd be plenty discouraged if my business and belongings had just gone up in flames." Setting the last of the fallen cookware on the kitchen counter, Paige dusted off her hands and offered to help. Betty shook her head.

"No, I need to put all these pots and pans away before I do anything. And then I'm taking a break before cooking. Thanks, anyway." Betty ran the back of her forearm across her brow.

"I'll go see what Mist's up to," Paige said. "I need to talk to Clive anyway."

"About the sapphire article?"

"That and some other things. Maybe I can bring Mist back, and we can both help you," Paige suggested. "It'll get her mind off the café, and you can rest."

Leaving Betty to reorganize the kitchen, Paige headed to the gem gallery. She found Mist and Clive in the back office. Clive slouched in his desk chair and gnawed on his pencil's eraser as he scowled at papers on the top of his desk. Beside him, Mist sat upright in a straight-backed chair, eyes closed and hands folded in her lap. If Paige hadn't witnessed Mist's shakiness the morning after the fire, she would have supposed nothing in the world could rattle the ethereal girl's spirit.

Clive looked up as Paige entered and waved her over to the desk.

"We were just discussing that stack of ashes that used to be a building." Clive's tone was gruff.

"As well as future possibilities. There are always future possibilities." Mist spoke softly, her eyes still closed, which kept her from seeing Clive roll his eyes.

"Some people are just too dang optimistic," Clive grumbled. A wisp of a smile flitted across Mist's face as Clive spoke.

"So what brings you in here today? Chasing Yogos again? You know I've got some mighty fine ones in that display case up front."

Paige laughed. "You were born to be in sales, Clive. I just might buy one of those pretty pieces from you yet – you're just that convincing. But I came up to talk to you about that painting of yours."

"What painting?" Mist opened her eyes and looked at Paige. Clive answered Mist before Paige could.

"That painting on the front wall. I'm thinking to sell it, help get the café rebuilt."

Mist looked uncharacteristically concerned. "That's a beautiful piece, Clive. Soft. Realistic. Are you sure you want to part with it?"

"I'm not attached to it sentimentally or anything, so why not put it to good use? Anyway, it might not even be worth anything." Clive huffed.

"Exactly why I came by to see you, Clive," Paige said, giving Mist a reassuring glance. "I talked to my friend, Jake, in Jackson, and he suggested we send it to an art appraiser."

"Friend..." Mist whispered the word like a magic spell. Paige thought back to the surprise dinner with Jake at Moonglow and smiled. Mist wasn't fooled by Paige's casual use of the term "friend."

"You going on about art appraisers again?" Clive looked dubious.

"Yes," Paige continued. "But we wouldn't have to send the painting all the way to New York. Jake knows an appraiser who works in Cody, at that Buffalo Bill Historical Center. I think it's worth sending the painting out there, have it looked at. I'd hate to see a buyer take advantage of you."

"Seems like a lot of commotion," Clive said. "Why not just advertise that it was painted by a student of Russell's and get what we can, based on that?"

"What?" Mist sat forward, leaning toward Clive. "Who says it was painted by a student of Charles Russell?"

Clive looked puzzled. "That's how I got it, Mist. It was in the basement of the café when I cleaned it out for you."

"But why would it be there?"

"Because that's where Russell's student had his studio. I thought you knew that."

Mist shook her head. "No, I had no idea."

Clive snorted as he filed another invoice into a folder for unpaid bills. "Well, don't feel too devastated, Mist. That studio workspace belonged to Silas Wheeler, a man of questionable talent and zero respect for his fellow man."

"Which brings us back to the question of value," Paige said, jumping right back into the conversation. "Let me help you find out what that painting of yours is worth. If it can help rebuild Moonglow, that's great. If it can't, it can't. At least you'll know you tried." She watched Clive thinking it over and knew he was leaning her way.

"Alright," Clive said. Standing, he crossed the room, lifted the painting off the wall and handed it to Paige. "Pack it up and send it off. No harm in finding out, I suppose."

CHAPTER EIGHTEEN

Paige jiggled the doorknob to her room, attempting to unlock it with one hand while reaching for her ringing cell phone with the other. As a result, the key slipped out of her hand and fell to the floor, along with the heavy binder of notes she'd been balancing between her arm and side. The phone was not far behind.

"You OK up there?" Betty's voice called up the staircase.

"I'm fine," Paige shouted back. "Just clumsy and trying to do too many things at once. Sorry for the disturbance." She gathered the notes together and picked up the key, ignoring the phone, which had already stopped ringing. She could check voicemail once she got settled inside the room. Now focused on the door alone, it easily opened. She set the binder and notes down on the writing table, put the room key on top of the dresser and retrieved the phone from the hallway floor, cautious to block the door to her room open with one foot while reaching awkwardly for the phone with her upper body. Finally gathering herself together, she closed the door and fell back on the bed.

It had been three days since shipping off the painting. With Jake back in Jackson, working on the ranch, she'd labored over the article, still bland without an interesting angle. Between writing spells, she'd exhausted herself trying to console Mist and help Betty feed the constantly gathering townsfolk.

The soft bedding was so comfortable that she succumbed to the temptation to rest momentarily. One minute. Or two, at most.

Forty-five minutes later, she opened her eyes to find the room had grown dark. With the setting of the sun, the temperature had dropped quickly. She clicked on the bedside light and, with a few hasty steps, reached the radiator and turned it up. Only then did she remember the missed phone call. Checking the cell phone for messages, she found two calls from Jake. Dialing his number, she was surprised to hear him answer it on the first ring.

"I've been trying to reach you." Paige couldn't decide if Jake sounded annoyed or relieved.

"I fell asleep. I only planned to rest my eyes for a couple minutes, but two turned into forty-five."

"Well, this will wake you up." Jake sounded serious, which was enough to rid Paige of her remaining drowsiness.

"What's up?" Paige twisted the metal knob on the radiator to crank it up and moved to the writing table, wishing suddenly that she had a mug of hot cocoa.

"I had a call from Lambert earlier this afternoon."

"Great," Paige said. "What's his verdict on the value of the Silas Wheeler painting?"

Jake cleared his throat, a stalling gesture in people that always triggered Paige's impatience.

"That's the thing," Jake said. "He seemed puzzled by the painting and said he needed more time to inspect it."

Paige's attention was now fully focused. "More time? He said it should only take a day to inspect."

"Right," Jake agreed. "But apparently there are inconsistencies. At least that's what he said today."

"What kind of inconsistencies?" Already she was out of her chair and pacing.

"Paige, you're asking the wrong person. If you want information on breeds of horses, I can help you out. But if you want educated evaluations of fine art, you're going to have to stick to Professor Lambert." Jake laughed, but Paige imagined that it was his turn to be annoyed with her.

"I'm sorry." Paige apologized, knowing she'd sounded pushy. "You're doing me a favor, having him look at it. I just get eager for answers." It was true. She had always been impatient, even as a young child. She hadn't changed. She found waiting for answers as frustrating as ever. She sighed and sat back down.

"Patience," Jake said. His smooth voice calmed her. He was solid and grounded, and she could always lean on him when she felt shaky. It was a good feeling.

"Yes – a virtue that has evaded me most of my life." She took a deep breath and looked out the window, a little more composed now. Two young boys roughhoused on the back property. A few late-clinging, crumpled leaves fell to the ground as a gust of wind whipped through. It was a peaceful scene outside, yet her curiosity would not rest.

Again, she began to pace. This could be bad news for Clive. If the painting wasn't valuable, he'd have to find another way to cover the insurance deductible on the café. Even if he waited until spring to rebuild, his business was too slow for him to save the necessary funds in time.

"When will we know more?" Paige gave the radiator a kick, holding one hand over it to check for heat. She was relieved to feel it warming up.

"Lambert said a few more days. He's having another Silas Wheeler painting sent down from Great Falls so he can compare the two side by side," Jake said. "If you're up for a long drive, I can meet you in Cody to go over the results with Lambert at his office when he's done with the analysis."

"I don't mind a long drive," Paige said. "I'd like to meet him and hear his explanation." Besides, she added to herself, it was a chance to see Jake again.

"How did another painting of Wheeler's turn up in Great Falls?" Paige asked.

"A woman from Helena donated it to the museum there, thinking it was a Charles Russell original. The curator realized it was by Silas Wheeler and had it set aside in basement storage."

"I guess I'll just have to be patient and wait a few more days for him to finish analyzing the paintings," Paige sighed.

She could hear Jake's muffled laugh on the other end of the phone.

"Yes, I know it's a challenge, but I'll do my best!"

After ending the call with Jake, Paige tried to focus on the sapphire mining article, but found her mind wandering back to the painting. She tried to picture it as it had appeared on the gallery wall, before she sent it to Cody for appraisal. It was a peaceful landscape scene, yet filled with the magnificent movement of horses. She could visualize the bright touches of blue dispersed throughout the skyline, as well as patches of red, orange and yellow around the covered wagon and campfire in the valley below. Despite her lack of art knowledge, the painting had spoken to her. Yet everything she heard about Silas Wheeler was laced with disrespect. Did he have more talent than people realized? Did his arrogance cause art critics to be particularly harsh with him?

Paige went downstairs to find Betty hard at work in the hotel kitchen. Two large pots sat on the stove; biscuit mix dusted the counter, and bowls of vegetables filled the center table. Paige picked up a handful of carrots and started in with a peeler she found.

"You can't feed the whole town by yourself, you know."

"You're supposed to be a guest here." Betty's words were sterner than her appearance. She looked like spring in her yellow floral-print dress that served as a backdrop for a bright green apron with a wild pattern of overlapping roosters and vegetables. When Paige looked at Betty's clothes, she imagined kitchen curtains might have flown off a window and draped themselves around Betty's neck and waist.

"But I want to help," Paige said.

It was true, she realized as she spoke, not only because she couldn't focus on writing the newspaper article, but because the townsfolk of Timberton were beginning to feel like friends. What was it about these small, western towns that she liked? Was it that they felt so much more personal than the big city? She continued to feel increasingly drawn to this way of life.

"I'm going down to Cody in a couple of days," Paige said. "But I'll keep my room. I may just make it a day trip."

"Cody, you say, as in Wyoming?" Betty smiled. "That's quite a day trip. Maybe you're meeting up with a friend?"

Paige laughed. "I know what you're getting at, Betty. Yes, I'm meeting Jake. But that's not the reason for the trip. I want to hear firsthand what his art expert friend has to say about Clive's painting."

"Well, I hope for Clive's sake the guy has good news," Betty said. "Heck of a shame having the café burn down – for Clive, for Mist and for the whole town."

"Speaking of Mist, is she around?" Paige asked. She watched Betty rinse her hands under the faucet before drying them on her apron.

"She went over to the park to check on Hollister," Betty replied, waving her arm vaguely in the direction of the front hallway. "Wants him to know she'll bring him food later."

"Will he understand?" Paige scooped up a pile of carrot skins and threw them in the trash, bending down to pick up a few strays that missed the wastebasket.

"Who knows?" Betty sighed. "Every now and then there's a hint of focus in his eyes. But, for the most part, he just pokes that stick around in the dirt, picks up pebbles and stares into space."

Paige drummed her fingers on the tabletop. Her impatience was getting to her again. There were so many questions in this town and so few answers. She turned back to the stack of peeled carrots, sized them up and began to chop them into stew-sized chunks.

CHAPTER NINETEEN

Professor Lambert motioned for Paige and Jake to come closer. On a projected screen, two images of Clive's painting rested side by side. The photo to the right bore the most resemblance to the original painting. The one on the left differed. It was the same image, but with additional markings not visible in the photo on the right.

Paige moved closer, bending forward to compare the two images.

"I'm not sure what I'm looking at here. I apologize, but my art knowledge is weak and my understanding of scientific methods even weaker."

Professor Lambert adjusted the images and pointed first to the one on the right.

"This is a photograph of your painting, taken with a normal camera. It shows the scene just as you see it with the naked eye – colors, shapes, markings. It is merely a representation of the painting as it presents itself."

He stepped back, allowing Paige to study the photo. She took in the image, shifting her attention back and forth between the photos and the actual painting, which sat on an easel to the right.

"I don't see anything unusual," Paige said. "Is there supposed to be some discrepancy, and I'm just missing it?"

"Not at all." Again, Professor Lambert adjusted both photos and pointed to the one on the right. "Let me explain." He turned to face Paige and Jake, clearly pleased to have an audience. For a moment, Paige flashed back to science classes, prepared not to understand anything she was about to hear.

"The human eye is only capable of seeing certain wavelengths. The photo on your right displays what the original painting shows, nothing more. The paint is opaque. You can't see through it."

Paige nodded politely. "I see." Jake shot her a sideways look and grinned. She shrugged her shoulders when they made eye contact. She didn't really see at all and knew Jake was onto her.

Lambert continued, indicating the photo on the left.

"This is the same painting, except this image was taken using infrared reflectography. It allows us to see through the layers of paint that are opaque to the human eye. This technology records longer wavelengths. It lets us view what is below the painted surface."

"Which is?" Paige was trying to follow, but wasn't sure where the professor was headed with all this. The photos looked almost the same to her, though the one on the left seemed a bit blurred or bumpy.

"Do you see these lines?" Lambert indicated the rounded exterior of the covered wagon, several markings within the flames of a campfire and a curved line under the painting's signature. Looking closely, Paige saw what he was pointing out.

"Yes, they look like outlines. Very faint, like sketches."

"Exactly. These are what we call underdrawings. They're outlines an artist uses, often sketched in black on a clean, white canvas. Carbon absorbs light and reflects it. Though we can't see the markings through the upper paint layers ourselves, the infrared camera picks them up. Through the photo created by the reflectography process, we can see how an artist sets up outlines for a scene."

Paige rubbed her forehead. The professor's speech was leading somewhere, but she had no idea where.

"How does this help us know the value of the painting? It's still the same piece of artwork regardless of whatever outlines the artist used."

Lambert nodded, not bothering to hide a cat-that-ate-the-canary grin. "That's why we're lucky to have these tools now. We've only had infrared technology since the late 1960s. Before then, we could scrape the surface of a painting or inspect it from a variety of aspects. But we couldn't see through the layers to expose the underdrawings. And they tell us a lot."

"Such as?"

"I'm glad you asked!" Lambert looked pleased at the progress the session was making. Indicating a painting on a different easel, he continued. "I had this sent down from Great Falls, to compare it with the painting from your friend's gallery. It's similar, isn't it?"

Paige nodded. "It's not the same scene, but it has the same feeling. Same colors, background, sky, that sort of thing." Paige leaned in closer. "Are you saying this was also painted by Silas Wheeler?"

"Well, your statement is correct, except you'll need to remove the word 'also'."

Paige reworded her phrasing. "This was... painted by Silas Wheeler."

Lambert nodded. "That is correct."

"Now I'm confused." Paige walked over to the painting from the gallery, looked at it closely and returned to the new one from Great Falls. "This one was painted by Silas Wheeler."

"Yes, it was."

"But the painting we sent down from Clive's gallery was by Silas Wheeler."

Lambert shook his head. "I'm afraid not."

Paige's spirits plummeted. Clive was depending on the piece having value. He was counting on it, so he could start rebuilding the café.

"This is not good news," Paige sighed. Jake draped an arm around her, and she leaned against him for support.

"On the contrary, it's quite good news." Lambert appeared proud of himself. Paige and Jake mirrored each other's perplexed expressions.

"Let me explain." Lambert walked back over to the piece from the gallery. "I did some research on Silas Wheeler. Not the nicest guy, from what I've read, by the way. He was a student of Charles Russell, as you already know. He never gained much attention for his work. He believed himself to be as great a painter as Russell, but he wasn't. Wheeler's paintings never brought much money, nor did they bring the painter much respect. It didn't help that no one liked him. But the bottom line was, he just didn't have the talent."

"But you got that painting from the museum in Great Falls." Paige pointed back to the second painting. "And you say Silas Wheeler painted it. I'm trying to put this together."

Paige alternated glances between the paintings. "Clive said he got his painting from the basement of the building that is...I mean, was...the café. And that building was once Silas Wheeler's studio. He also signed Clive's painting."

Lambert nodded. "Yes, he signed this one and that one from Great Falls."

"So maybe they are both his, after all."

"One would think so, by the signatures, which were, indeed, both Wheeler's. But this is where the infrared photo tells a different story. The underdrawings on the one from your friend's gallery are quite different from those on the actual Wheeler painting."

Paige paused before speaking. "Clive said Wheeler's earlier paintings were poor quality, but improved later in his life. Improved dramatically, in fact."

"Yes, I can see by comparing these two that they did." Lambert laughed. "And there's a good reason for that, which we now know from the infrared analysis."

"Which is?" Both Paige and Jake asked the question at the same time.

"It's because, quite simply, he didn't paint them. He signed the later paintings, but someone else painted them."

"So you're saying he passed off someone else's paintings as his own?"

"That's exactly what I'm saying."

"Then who painted this one?" Paige indicated Clive's painting.

Lambert shrugged. "Someone very talented. But who? I have no idea."

CHAPTER TWENTY

Paige leaned against the back of the booth and watched Jake order a glass of Chardonnay for her and a draft beer for himself. The waitress set two cocktail napkins on the table, fringe swinging forward from the hem of her cropped, denim vest as she did so. Dangling silver earrings in the shape of cowboy hats mimicked the motion of the fringe. Paige watched the twenty-something server walk away from the table. The dining room's décor was extravagant.

"So this is the Irma Hotel," Paige said.

Jake nodded. "That it is, built in 1902 by Buffalo Bill. He called it 'just the sweetest hotel that ever was.' Named it after his youngest daughter. And a fine place it is, too." Jake took a swig of his beer and looked around the room, clearly proud.

Paige took in the high, tin ceiling, the expansive sea of dining tables and, finally, the massive cherry wood bar that ran the length of the far wall.

"I've never seen a bar like that."

Jake laughed. "And you can bet you never will, at least not anywhere else. That was a gift from Queen Victoria to Buffalo Bill. That bar traveled all the way from England, no small feat in those days."

"I can't even imagine. How would you even get something like that over here?" Paige couldn't take her eyes off the intricate carving and rich tone of the wood.

"Slowly, I figure," Jake said. "First it had to travel by steamer, to get it across the Atlantic, then by railroad, which would get it to Montana, and then by horse-drawn carriage the rest of the way down here to Cody,"

"Why would she give him a gift like that? What was the connection?"

"That's easier to answer. Buffalo Bill's western show, known as 'Buffalo Bill's Wild West,' toured Europe for years. His first overseas performances were in Great Britain, including one or more command performances for the queen."

Paige sipped her wine and nodded – a combination of movements that turned out to be less than graceful. Jake pressed his fingers against his mouth to cover his smirk.

Jake glanced at his watch and changed the subject. "How about something to eat? Best buffet in town is right here."

"He's got that right," the fringe-toting waitress chipped in. She overheard Jake's comment while she finished up an order at the booth behind theirs. "Prime rib, buffalo stew, baked ham, mashed potatoes..."

"Salad?" Paige managed a meek whisper.

"Yep, that too," the server said. "I'll put you guys down for two buffets. Help yourselves and just holler if you need another round of drinks."

Over generous plates of food, Paige and Jake settled back into conversation, but switched gears. They'd set aside discussing the meeting with Professor Lambert while they absorbed the history and ambience of the Irma, but now their questions returned.

"I don't know what to think about Lambert's conclusions." Jake was frowning and Paige wasn't sure if it was because he was concerned about the art or just frustrated with an attempt to negotiate the best ratio of horseradish to prime rib.

Paige speared a forkful of greens and responded. "I'm as confused as you are. I thought having the painting appraised would make things more clear. Instead it seems we have a whole new dilemma."

"Lambert said he'd dig a little deeper and see if he could find something out. Maybe he'll identify the real painter."

Paige sighed. "I don't know if that will do any good, at this point. The painting must date back to the same time period that Silas was alive, since the signature is his. So it's likely this new mystery painter is dead."

"Probably true," Jake agreed. "But that doesn't lessen the value. Maybe Lambert's search will turn up other pieces by the same painter. They could analyze other paintings that Silas signed now that the infrared test has shown at least one is someone else's work."

"It would make sense that there were more, then." Paige paused and set her fork down. "If there are, and the quality is as outstanding as Lambert made it sound, Clive could be looking at some decent money."

"Maybe," Jake said. "Or Silas may have just found a painting that was similar to his style and decided to put his name on it. Don't get your hopes up. This could just be a fluke."

Paige sighed. "You don't think this painting of Clive's is worth anything."

"I didn't say that." Jake set his fork down, too, and reached across the table to squeeze Paige's hand. "I just don't want you to be disappointed if this turns out to be no more than a conceited, mediocre artist's prank."

Jake returned to the buffet for another serving. Paige took advantage of the break in conversation to check her cell phone. There were two messages, one from Clive and the other from the New York office. Clive's was short, just asking if she'd found anything out about the painting. The other was even shorter – Susan, asking Paige to call in an update.

An update? That would take some sorting out to put together. The meeting with Lambert had thrown a new twist into the painting puzzle, not that Susan was aware of her side step into the world of western art. And the sapphire article still needed more work. More focus on Paige's part, to be specific.

Jake slid back into the booth with another slab of prime rib, a baked potato and a side of green beans. He took a look at his plate, stalled before picking up his knife and fork and gave Paige a sheepish grin.

"My grandmother would have said my eyes were bigger than my stomach," he muttered.

"You don't have to finish it all."

"Pretty doubtful I will. Especially with apple cobbler up there, just waiting."

Paige's eyes lit up. "Now I could go for a few bites of that. I knew there was a reason I stuck to the salad bar." After a quick trip to the buffet, she was back in the booth with a diminutive serving of the homemade dessert.

"You shouldn't drive all the way back to Timberton tonight, you know." Jake's expression was half-flirtatious and half-serious.

"I was thinking about that," Paige said. "I'd be back in Timberton by midnight, but I'll admit I'm starting to feel the day catch up to me." She took a bite of cobbler, closing her eyes to appreciate the sweet, baked apples and flaky cinnamon-ginger crust. The waitress passed by briefly, refilling water glasses and dropping a check down on the table. Jake tossed a credit card on it and held up his hand, signaling for Paige not to argue about paying the bill.

"There's lodging back near the Buffalo Bill Historical Center. I saw it when I drove in. Or they may have rooms here." Paige looked around appreciatively at the historical building. "Probably old-fashioned and full of character."

"I have a better idea." Jake had mischief in his eyes.

"And what would that be?" Paige tried to play it casual, but felt a flush creep up her neck.

"Let me make a phone call. I have connections here, you know."

"Well, I should think so," Paige laughed. "You lived here most of your life, right?"

"Yep. Just about my whole life, until I moved to Jackson."

Jake set his fork down and pushed his plate away in surrender. "That apple cobbler's gonna have to wait for another time." He pulled his cell phone out, indicated the door while motioning for Paige to relax, and headed outside to make a call. Within a few minutes he was back in the booth.

"That was quick," Paige pointed out.

"Just checking with an old family friend who has a guest ranch outside of town. Said he's got rooms open and to come on out."

"Well, this is your territory, so I'll go with whatever you suggest." Again Paige felt her neck grow warm.

"It's about ten miles outside of town. We could ride out there together or you could follow me."

"I'd rather not leave the rental car here in town," Paige said.

"Just follow me out there, then. It's pretty much a straight shot. Most of it is even paved." Jake grinned.

"Most of it?" Paige raised her eyebrows, concerned.

Jake laughed. "This is country, my dear big city girl. But only the last mile is unpaved. You'll be fine. We'll just slow down on that final stretch."

CHAPTER TWENTY-ONE

Despite her experiences of nighttime in Timberton, Paige was shocked at the pitch-blackness that surrounded her as soon as she hit the outskirts of Cody. If she hadn't been following Jake's truck, she would have crawled along at a snail's pace. It was like driving through a dark tunnel. A faint, dotted line ran down the middle of the road. Aside from that, there was nothing. She could have been driving between tall mountains, or the land beyond the road could have dropped off into a deep canyon. There was no way to tell.

Miles passed by as she followed Jake's taillights. Each unexpected bump in the road sent a shiver up her spine. Periodically her headlights allowed a glimpse of a bush near the edge of the road or a tree limb perched above. Fearful for the area's wildlife, she braked often, accelerating afterwards to keep up with Jake. Consciously, she knew she wasn't far from town and had a trusty guide in front of her. But the dark, visual unknown unsettled her.

To steady her nerves, she reviewed the information she'd gathered since arriving in Timberton. The residents of the old mining town seemed unconnected at first glance. Yet the longer she stayed and the better she got to know them, the more their individual stories intertwined. Perhaps they simply shared a common geography and long-time residency. But it seemed like more.

Clive owned the sapphire gallery, yet also owned the building where Moonglow had been located. Silas Wheeler had used that building as a studio, but had lived in the hotel, now run by Betty. Wheeler's studio later became the café, run by Mist, also an artist. Clive's painting, found in the café basement, was supposedly by Wheeler, but now appeared to be another artist's work. It all formed a complicated web. One thing was clear: Timberton held more secrets than met the eye.

Paige's thoughts were interrupted by a sudden jolt as her tires hit the first few feet of unpaved road. Had she been paying attention to driving, she might have seen the change in the road's surface coming. Instead, she gasped in surprise, hit the brakes and felt the car skid a few yards before coming to a stop. Jake's brake lights grew brighter as he slowed down. It was reassuring to know he wasn't leaving her behind. She took a deep, calming breath, regrouped and stepped on the accelerator. As she resumed her driving, Jake did the same.

The jarring sound of loose gravel hitting the bottom of her car, combined with the surrounding darkness, proved nerve-racking. The mile of unpaved road felt like five miles. She was relieved to finally spy a dull glow of lights up ahead off to the right. As she expected, Jake's truck veered in that direction. She followed him, and the lights grew brighter, eventually establishing themselves as the window lights of an old ranch house. She pulled up alongside Jake's truck as he parked, turned off the ignition and stepped out of the car.

"This is Jeb Barkley's place," Jake said. "He grew up with my father, been an old family friend for as long as I can remember. He runs this property as a guest ranch. Makes a pretty good living off of it during the summer months. Right now it's darn quiet."

Paige stretched her arms over her head, glad to be out of the confines of the vehicle. "I saw a sign back where we turned off the road, but couldn't read it."

"That's the ranch sign, says Circle B Ranch. He keeps the light off during the off-season. Not that anyone's likely to be way out here to find it by chance."

"That's for sure," Paige mumbled. The night was so black even the road they'd driven in on seemed to have disappeared.

Jake pulled a duffle bag out of his truck and let the door swing shut, sending an echo out into the void. "C'mon, I'll introduce you to Jeb. He'll give us a quick tour and leave us be. He's probably happily curled up by the fireplace with a good book right now."

After the drive down from Timberton, the session with Lambert and the meal at The Irma, a good book in front of a fire sounded appealing to Paige. But, then again, there was Jake. A quick wisp of air escaped her lips. The two of them had managed to end up together at a remote ranch with the night stretching ahead.

"Cold?" Jake threw out the question casually, knowing that Paige would say she was fine, whether she was or not.

"No, just taking everything in." Paige pulled her overnight bag from the trunk of the rental car, dropped the lid to close it and followed that with a sharp, electronic beep.

The sound drew an immediate burst of laughter from Jake. "Paige, did I just hear you lock the car?" Paige smiled in the dark, but didn't respond.

"We don't allow the coyotes out here to have drivers' licenses, you know. And a bison would need a bigger car than a Hyundai Accent."

Paige accepted the teasing. "Go ahead, make fun of me. A habit is a habit, that's all." She paused before adopting a feigned tone of seriousness and adding, "After all, you have those jackalopes out here, and one of them would easily fit behind the wheel."

"Catching up on your western folklore, I see." Jake ran his hand across the small of Paige's back and gently motioned her toward the front door.

CHAPTER TWENTY-TWO

The main house of the Circle B Ranch was breathtaking, like something straight out of a western design magazine. As Jake predicted, Jeb Barkley was sitting in front of the fireplace, a book nestled between his hands. A handsome man in his mid-60s, his rugged, western demeanor hinted he could impress the ladies, on or off a horse.

Paige was so impressed with the room, she could barely focus on saying hello to their host. The vaulted pine ceiling easily rose thirty feet into the air. One sole, multi-layered antler chandelier hovered halfway between the wooden flooring and ceiling peak. Complementary antler sconces were scattered on the walls in just enough places to give the room a warm glow without over-lighting it. Clusters of soft, leather furniture formed subsets of social spaces. Paige could imagine vacationing family members playing cards in one section while other guests lounged with glasses of wine in another. Yet smaller areas offered quiet places for readers to sink into good books. A well-stocked bookcase rested against one wall.

The windows were impressive, as well, soaring high above the comfortable room. Even with nothing but black night beyond them, Paige could sense the open land and big sky outside.

"Nice surprise, Jake. About time you came back to Cody and paid your old friends a visit." Jeb stood up, set his book aside and extended a sturdy handshake to Jake before turning to Paige.

"And who do we have here?" Jeb raised his eyebrows and offered Paige his most welcoming smile.

"Paige MacKenzie, meet Jeb Barkley. And watch out for him, he's a genuine sweet-talkin' cowboy." Jake and Jeb exchanged joking arm punches. Paige shook her head, amused at the male shenanigans.

"Mighty pleased to have you here, Ms. MacKenzie." Jeb straightened up and tipped an imaginary hat, accompanied by a subtle wink.

"Just 'Paige' is fine, Mr. Barkley."

"In that case, just call me 'Jeb.' We're not that formal around these parts." Jeb indicated a cowhide couch with overstuffed throw pillows in muted earth tones. Paige and Jake moved to the sitting area. The crackling fire in the fireplace was a welcome sight after the dark drive out from Cody.

"What brings you out this way? Showing Ms. MacKenzie...I mean Paige...your old stomping grounds?" Jeb threw his head back and let out a hearty laugh before turning toward Paige. "And let me tell you, this guy did some stomping in his time."

"OK, Jeb, we probably don't need to go down that particular road." Jake's voice interrupted Jeb's statement, but he took the light-hearted teasing well.

"Oh, I think we do," Paige said quickly, grinning at Jake mischievously. "I'd love to hear a few stories."

Jeb settled back in his chair and rubbed his forehead in a mock gesture of mentally dredging up the past. It was clear he had a good stash of material. It was only a matter of choosing between episodes. Jake, resigned to what was coming, leaned back and waited for the inevitable.

"Well now, Jake's father – may he rest in peace – and I go back a long ways. He was the first friend I made when I moved out here from Nebraska as a boy. Taught me a lot about the Cody way of life. Made me feel welcome."

Jeb paused, if for no other reason than to make Jake wonder what was coming next. Jake didn't have to wait long.

"Back then, Jake was just a little tyke, about five years old. Cute as a button and determined to be a real cowboy. And...he had quite the dramatic streak in him, too, a regular John Wayne in miniature."

Jake winced. Paige knew whatever was coming must be good. She smiled at Jeb and motioned with her hand for him to go on.

Jeb looked smug and pleased with his captive audience, not to mention his kind-hearted position of control over Jake. He paused again, for effect.

"Go on, Jeb," Jake said, "get it over with. There's no stopping you once you get started. I knew I was taking my chances when I called about coming out here."

"You're right about that," Jeb said. He laughed as he turned back to Paige.

"So, you probably know our town here was founded by Buffalo Bill Cody. He was a man of vision and a great entertainer, formed a marvelous show that traveled all over the world, just about."

"Buffalo Bill's Wild West Show, right?" Paige interjected.

Jeb shook his head. "Almost right. It was called 'Buffalo Bill's Wild West.' People just tend to add the word 'show,' but it was never part of the name."

"Like Smokey the Bear," Paige offered.

"Exactly," Jeb nodded in approval.

Seeing Jake's confused look, Paige explained. "It was always Smokey Bear, never Smokey *the* Bear. But people get used to hearing and saying things one way and it sticks."

"Anyway," Jeb cleared his throat to bring attention back to the story. "Little Jake was enamored with Buffalo Bill and was convinced he was going to grow up to be just like his idol. He collected pictures of him and kept a scrapbook. He practiced posing like those pictures, standing in front of the mirror and putting on his best Buffalo Bill face. Made everyone call him Buffalo Jake. He was darn cute, that little wannabe cowboy."

"I'm sure he was." Paige loved the look of resignation on Jake's face. It made him all the sweeter.

"Well, all that pretending wasn't enough," Jeb went on. "Jake decided he needed to have a show, just like Buffalo Bill. He gathered kids from other ranches and assigned roles, thought up little skits and rehearsed them. He was very serious about it. And he had that entrepreneur spirit of Buffalo Bill's, too, drawing posters to advertise the shows. Of course, they couldn't use any horses, being little tykes like he and his friends were. But they used ranch dogs and got them to do tricks. It was quite impressive."

"How I'd love to see a video of that," Paige laughed.

"I'm glad there isn't one." Jake shook his head, ready for the story to be over.

"What eventually happened to this illustrious show?"

Jeb sighed in mock sadness. "The ensemble was torn apart by the start of the school year. Young actors and actresses were scattered in all directions, taken hostage by the town's first-grade teachers. Show biz gave way to education. It was a cryin' shame."

"Indeed, it was," Jake proclaimed. "As was telling this tale to begin with, Jeb."

Jeb stood up and stretched, pleased with himself. He tucked the book he'd been reading before their arrival under his arm.

"I'm glad you're here, Buffalo Jake. And you too, Ms. Paige MacKenzie, newest fan of Buffalo Jake's Wild West. But it's time for this old rancher to call it a night. Jake, you know the layout. There aren't any other guests here tonight. It's been slow this off-season. So you have your choice of rooms. Feel free to give Paige a tour and settle in wherever you want. There's beer and wine in the kitchen and firewood out back. I'll whip something up for breakfast in the morning. Just don't expect any of that fancy bed and breakfast type cuisine." Jeb tipped his imaginary hat once again and was gone.

The spacious room felt oddly silent once Jeb was gone, and Jake and Paige were left on their own. Without their host's jovial personality, an uncertain silence hung in the air. To break the tension, both Paige and Jake spoke simultaneously.

"I'll get firewood from the back."

"I'll bring those notes in from the meeting today with Lambert."

Heading in opposite directions, they met up again in front of the fireplace. Paige sat and flipped through her notes while Jake tossed new logs on the fire and adjusted them with the poker.

"How does a glass of wine sound?" Jake stood back to admire the growing flames.

"Sounds great." Paige looked up from her notes and smiled. As it had many times before, the sight of Jake's lean, relaxed body stoked her feelings. The reflection of the fire settled on his tanned face with a deep, warm glow and danced through his hair like fireflies in the night.

"Red or white? I'm sure he has both."

"White would be perfect." And it might calm my nerves, Paige added silently.

Jake sauntered to the kitchen, his cowboy boots clicking casually against the Circle B Ranch's wooden floor. He returned with two chilled glasses of Chardonnay, handed one to Paige and sat next to her.

"I thought you were more of a beer drinker," Paige said as they brought the shimmering glasses together in a toast.

Jake laughed and gave Paige a look she couldn't quite decipher. "You're right, but wine seemed more in line with this evening's atmosphere: the luxury ranch, the fireplace, you, here with me."

Paige caught her breath. Had she been afraid of this, coming back out west? The draw that she had felt toward Jake originally, in Jackson, was only growing stronger. Two thousand miles separated them most of the time, Wyoming and New York worlds apart. Other than the series of western articles for work, there was no way to know when they'd be able to see each other.

Jake was just inches away, and Paige decided to push aside her conflicted feelings. She sipped her wine. Time and distance might be obstacles in the future, but at that moment, one thing was certain: tonight there were no obstacles between them.

* * * *

Hours later, Paige leaned against a log post on the ranch porch, sleepless but happy. Through her plush, terrycloth robe, the solid wood of the post reminded her of Jake's strong, but gentle, hands caressing her face. She hardly felt the snow flurries that fell on her cheeks. Was the snow in New York the same as this? Or did Wyoming have its own secret winter formula? The wispy flakes were so light, so free. They sparkled in the night air, backlit by the faint glow of the lodge's exterior lighting. They swirled upwards, sideways, downwards, like tiny, transparent ribbons. Windswept, they brushed against her skin like a waterfall's mist and melted. She closed her eyes and listened to the night: wind, an owl's hoot, the distant howl of a coyote. All so quiet yet the potential was nearly audible

Potential. Yes, that was it, the reason the snow seemed different from the snow back home.

CHAPTER TWENTY-THREE

The morning drive back to Timberton seemed short despite the many miles. Paige had always been able to organize her thoughts when she drove long distances. But this time, she couldn't focus on the new information they'd acquired from Lambert. Memories of last night pushed everything else aside. When she remembered the warm tones in Clive's painting, she thought of the flames in the Circle B Ranch's fireplace. The colors of the painting's cool, blue sky reminded her of Jake's eyes. She had become a hopeless romantic.

Paige pulled up in front of the hotel, turned off the ignition and set the parking brake. The light snow of the previous Wyoming night had evolved into a sunny Montana afternoon. She needed to focus on the sapphire article and on helping Mist, Clive and Betty.

The lobby was vacant when she entered the hotel. Upstairs, Paige soon had her overnight bag unpacked, and within minutes, she was seated at the desk, reviewing notes from the meeting with Lambert. Although the new information about the painting didn't provide anything conclusive, at least it was something to report to Clive.

As for the sapphire article, she had nothing new for Susan. Her side trip to Cody had cost her twenty-four hours, an indulgence that put added pressure on her for finishing the article. Her rough draft was done, but it *was* rough.

Two hours and three cups of coffee later, she had made little progress. She stood, stretched and moved to the edge of the bed, pulling out the partial diary. Reading over the few pages again only fueled her curiosity. With the hotel still quiet, she could try to search the room below hers. She stepped out in the hallway, eased the door shut behind her and went downstairs.

The door to the laundry area was propped open with an over-sized, canvas hamper. Two washing machines, lids resting open against the wall, edged the room. Scratches on the enamel surfaces recounted decades of activity. On the adjacent wall, one of two dryers hummed as linens tumbled inside the glass door. Wooden shelves above held laundry supplies. Faded curtains framed the sole window, which was covered with condensation. Clusters of lint dusted the floor. Brooms and mops leaned against a corner.

A wave of humidity and the scent of fabric softener enveloped Paige as she stepped inside the room. She glanced up, noted the ceiling and the distance between the doorway and the walls. The room was a straight fit below the one she occupied as a guest. She gathered her bearings and determined the location that would be directly below the radiator in her room. Just to the left of the rumbling dryer – that was the likely spot. She placed the palm of her hand flat against the wall's surface. Warmth reflected back against her skin, as if greeting her with a familiar friendship.

She tapped the wall lightly with her fingers, hearing a hollow echo within. Her eyes followed the wall upward, stopping at the point where it joined the ceiling. Looking to the side wall, she estimated the distance. This had to be where the torn portion of the diary had fallen, directly below her room.

She searched the wall's surface for an opening, but found nothing. There were no built-in shelves or cabinets that might have an interior board or panel to pry loose. Pressing the side of her face against the wall, she inspected the area behind the dryer. A crumbling patch of wallboard looked promising, but revealed only splintered wood and cobwebs inside. And the dryer vented off to the side. Even if she were to remove the vent and search behind it, the location was too far away. It was unlikely anything falling inside the wall could have angled sharply off a straight downward path. Short of breaking right through the wall itself, she was out of luck.

"Have you lost something?"

Paige jumped at the sound of Mist's voice behind her. She straightened up too quickly, and her head smacked the low shelving and sent a jug of liquid detergent crashing to the floor. Surprisingly, the container did not explode into a soapy flood. It merely bounced with a dull thud and came to rest, rocking slightly, beside Mist, who glanced at it so casually, it might have been a feather falling from the sky. Mist turned away, occupied with loading a basket full of kitchen linens into one of the washers.

"No," Paige stammered. "I was just...looking for..." What could she say she was looking for? She turned toward the shelving to stall for time, pushing back a bottle of bleach that was teetering precariously on the shelf's edge.

"Extra towels are over there."

Mist pointed to a cabinet beside the window, its doors open to reveal several rows of shelves.

Piles of neatly folded towels sat side by side, freshly laundered and ready for another round of use in guest rooms. Paige picked two from the top of the closest stack, hugged them to her chest and smiled a meek thank you. She left the room as quickly as Mist seemed to have arrived.

Paige took the stairs two at a time to her room, closed the door behind her with a soft click and a twist of the lock. She stacked the towels on top of two others just like them, still unused, and sat at the desk. Staring out the window, she took a quick mental inventory of the day, not satisfied with the results: too many towels, too little information.

As it stood, she couldn't be sure the missing diary pages were inside the laundry room wall. Just because they were out of arm's reach didn't mean they had fallen that far. After running into Mist, she'd had to abandon her search of the laundry room. But there was nothing stopping her from double-checking her own room. The question was how.

Slipping back down to the hotel lobby, she stepped behind the registration desk and fumbled through the back cabinets, keeping an ear out for sounds of other people. The first cabinet door revealed only haphazard file folders and memo pads. The second was empty, save for boxes of packaged sugars and creamers for morning coffee. But the third cabinet offered a handyman's jackpot. Suddenly a newly formed plan emerged. She gathered a loose bundle of twine, a roll of duct tape and two hammers and tiptoed back up the stairs to her room. It was a crazy plan, but worth a try.

Paige spread out the borrowed goods on her bed. She set the two hammers side by side, facing opposite directions, and wrapped them in layers of duct tape. The end result was an elongated, massive wad of tape with a hammerhead at each end. Grasping one metal claw, Paige looped the twine around it, tied a square knot and proceeded to wind the thick string around the hammer in crisscross fashion until it held the contraption securely. She let the length of twine out and held it in front of her. The taped hammers hung suspended in mid-air. It wasn't an engineering masterpiece, but it would do.

Paige reopened the space behind the radiator and slipped her bulky creation inside, holding tightly to the twine. The taped hammers dropped little more than a foot before coming to an abrupt halt at the floor level. She pulled them back out and reached inside the wall with her arm, feeling for the rotted area she had felt before. If she could find the narrow section that had been wide enough for the slim papers to fall through, she could use the weight of the hammers to widen it.

She prodded for a good thirty seconds before finding the gap in the floorboard. Pushing against it with her arm, the rotted segment of wood creaked and came close to giving in, but it wasn't enough. Pulling her arm out, she reached back in with the taped hammers and pushed again. This time the wood gave way. She continued to break through until she'd cleared a path several inches wide.

Dull thuds echoed back up as the hammers smacked against crossbeams. Each time Paige lowered and raised the makeshift tool, it brought up nothing more than rotted wood, and she felt ridiculous. Finally, she gave it one last try, letting the twine swing back and forth. Exhausted, she almost didn't notice when the swinging motion stopped. When she pulled the twine upward, she felt resistance. The claw of the lower hammer was caught on something.

Flashbacks to her first attempt at removing the diary reminded her of the pitfalls of being impatient. Paige angled the twine differently, pulling gently. Still, the hammers would not budge. She debated finagling yet another tool in hopes it could detach the one already stuck, but let out a frustrated laugh. That idea was just as ludicrous as what she was already trying.

She continued until she wore out. Legs shaking from hunching down so long, she didn't foresee the tumble coming. One minute she was leaning against the wall. The next, she was sprawled out on the floor, twine still wrapped around her hand. She glanced down. The fibers were cutting into her skin, but the weight against her hand had shifted. She began to reel in the twine, expecting to see only her crazy contraption at the end of the line. Instead, attached to the lower claw, was a cluster of papers. She knew the second she spotted it that it was another diary section.

The first dated entry was more than a decade later than those she'd found before.

March 8, 1955

I have found an exceptional student. There is clarity in his work that reminds me of C. More pointedly, it reminds me of who I could have been, had C. been a teacher who knew what to do with talent like my own. The credit I have always deserved is long overdue. This young man, this impressionable artist, may be very useful to me, both to my monetary existence and to my legacy.

After that, a section of torn pages followed and then two more entries.

April 22, 1959

Blessed miracle! A mishap today may have provided a solution for my recent fears. While trying to pry a nail from a cellar post, I lost my balance and fell backwards, sending the hammer flying over my head and into a wall. A crack resulted as the tool became wedged in the wall's surface. When I dislodged the hammer, the crack widened, and a chunk of wood fell forward. I could hardly believe my eyes – there was a space behind the wall! I grabbed the hammer and attacked the surface with a vicious fury. Surely, had anyone seen me, they would have thought me to be the maniac that my reputation around town claims me to be. But I hit the jackpot. Hidden behind that crumbling wall was a space large enough to hold a dozen paintings, if not more!

September 22, 1959
Tally: Landscapes (212 – 218) – 7, Tribal Conflicts (233 – 238) – 6, Covered Wagons (244 – 247)– 4, Horses – (261 – 265) 5, Bison (286 – 287) – 2, Maiden on Blanket (279) - 1, Dust Storm (293) – 1, Wolves (257 – 259) – 3, Winter Scenes (226 – 227) – 2

Pulling out the diary, she compared the pages to those still attached. Looking at the damaged, torn section, it made sense. The frustrated artist had destroyed much of what he'd recorded. Or had he?

She slid the pages into the diary and sighed. She would have to keep looking.

CHAPTER TWENTY-FOUR

Paige calculated the distance from Timberton to Great Falls and back. Betty and Mist had gone to buy supplies and ingredients for meals and would be gone for at least four hours, plenty of time for Paige to get into the basement and back out before they returned. Finding the key quickly would be important, which could pose a problem. She had no idea where Betty kept it, only that the basement was locked for the safety of guests until the rotted sections of the interior could be stabilized – just one of many needed repairs to the hotel.

The desk in the front lobby was the likely place to start. Downstairs, Paige stepped behind the heavy, mahogany counter and faced the back wall. The cubbyholes of the mail slots each held one or two keys. Since each compartment was numbered, it seemed clear those keys corresponded with guest rooms rather than the basement door. She ran her hand across the top of the highest shelf, but found nothing. She also found nothing when she peeked under the lowest row of compartments.

Paige studied the drawers below the counter. There were dozens of them, in all sizes – some slim enough to hold only a few sheets of letterhead, others deep enough for vertical file folders. The drawer handles were intricate in design and polished, in keeping with Betty's careful upkeep of the hotel's interior. Works of art, these built-in components of old hotels.

Pulling up Betty's desk chair, Paige settled into it and prepared for a detailed search. She searched the front counter and desk drawers for fifteen minutes without turning up anything more interesting than office supplies and hotel files, Betty's secret stash of caramels, a shawl and three romance novels. The discovery of Betty's personal items sent a ripple of guilt through Paige. She didn't mean to snoop, just to investigate, but she realized the line between these two behaviors was a fine one.

Paige stood back and placed her hands on her hips, fingers facing backwards. It was an odd pose that she fell into when frustrated, a childhood habit. A critical uncle had once told her it made her arms look like chicken wings, angular and out of alignment. Sometimes she stood this way just to spite him.

Paige took her search into the kitchen where she pulled open more drawers and found only the expected cooking utensils, pot holders and recipe cards. There was no sign of a key until she stood up straight and looked below the cupboards. Hanging on a hook next to the suspended coffee mugs was a key ring. She snagged the jangling cluster of metal and headed for the back hallway.

The overhead light was dim near the basement door. Paige fumbled around, inserting one key after another into the lock, but each key jammed halfway in. Reaching the end of the ring's circle, she went through the process again, this time forcing herself to maneuver the lock more delicately. The metal clattering of the keys grated against her. Finally one key slid in farther than the others. With one hand, she jiggled the doorknob while working the key with the other until the key slipped the rest of the way into the lock, and a twist of the knob opened the door.

The lighting above the basement stairs was even duller than it was in the hallway. Paige was relieved to find a switch just inside the door, feeble though the illumination was when she flipped it on. She stepped forward, reaching out to test a wooden handrail to her right. A light touch revealed the railing was too shaky to bear any weight. She withdrew her hand and focused on keeping her balance. The first few steps were sturdy, but others creaked underneath her as she descended the stairs, causing her to pause more than once. Each time she bolstered her nerves again and continued downward until she reached the bottom of the staircase.

The space was nearly the same size as her room, two floors above, just a few feet wider. Stacks of boxes, dusty shelves and abandoned appliances surrounded her. The old boiler, prone to periodic bursts of noise, stood in the far corner. She moved forward, shuffling her feet slowly across each rickety floorboard to make sure there was nothing to cause her to trip. The wooden slats rocked back and forth with each step, making it a challenge to keep her balance. A dank smell of dirt accosted her nostrils.

She found a flashlight on a worktable, switched it on and scanned the wall for openings. It was solid, as she expected. She swung the light up toward the ceiling, hoping to see an open vent, but found only old tools hanging from hooks, mixed in with a few dusty, ripped flour sacks. Something touched her cheek and she spun around to feel a cobweb wrap itself across her face. She shuddered as she wiped it off.

Paige refocused her attention across the dismal room. The boiler gurgled in that rumbling, deep tone she recognized as one of its many sporadic exclamations. It seemed more dramatic from her current perspective, certainly louder in the cellar than from two floors above. Perhaps the leak that Betty had referred to was what gave the fixture its varied repertoire. How old was it? One hundred years? More? It deserved to be cranky at that age, leak or no leak.

When she took a step forward and shifted her weight onto the next floorboard, it sounded like it snapped. She froze in place for a moment, then rocked her foot back and forth before she determined the board was stable and then continued. Two steps later, she felt her toe catch against something solid and lowered the flashlight's beam toward her foot. A second layer of planks had been placed above those closest to the boiler – reinforcement for the original flooring, Paige realized, eyeing the layer of damp, rotted wood below. Backing up this theory were heavy cables attached to the boiler and bolted to the brick wall, taking the weight of the heavy unit off the floor itself.

Paige was just musing that Betty needed to take care of the water damage and replace the old boiler with modern heating when another step resulted in a sharp crack. In what seemed like a split second, she felt the dry boarding slip beneath her, sending her knees into a slimy puddle of rotted wood. When she tried to stand, she slipped again, landing on her side this time. Determined, she propped one elbow up and was drawing herself up on her knees when she felt the decayed wood below her give out altogether. As mildewed mud slapped her face, and a thick, slurping filled her ears, she felt herself sliding downward. Grasping frantically, she caught the edge of a wooden beam, but couldn't hold on. Falling was all she remembered before blacking out.

CHAPTER TWENTY-FIVE

The first thing Paige felt when she came to was a throbbing pain. She lifted a shaky hand to her head to find a thick stream of liquid stuck to the side of her face. Blood.

Disoriented, she opened her eyes, blinked and fought to engage her senses. She was lying on her side. The air was cold, but not freezing, and there was no wind, no sound. The smell of damp earth surrounded her. Was she outside?

Paige struggled to sit up, which sent a flash of pain across her forehead. Shaking her arms and legs, she determined she hadn't broken any bones. But her head was bleeding. What had she hit it on? How far had she fallen? When she patted the ground around her, she felt dirt and gravel, but nothing else. She pulled her sweatshirt from around her waist and pressed it against her forehead. Removing it, she felt for the cut with her fingers and winced as she located it just inside the hairline. It was long, but shallow. The bleeding had stopped. How long had she been out?

She groped the area around her, and found the ground was uneven and piled with mud and debris. She jerked her arm back as a sharp spike stung her hand – a nail. Twisting, she reached out to search another direction, finding more of the same – dampened piles of dirt and splintered strips of wood. Finally her fingers landed on a solid object with a smooth finish. She wrapped her hands around its familiar shape and her heart leapt. It was the flashlight.

Its beam was dim but strong enough to help her take stock of her surroundings. She aimed it first at the ground and then upward, blinking with disbelief at the gaping hole above her. The faint glow and recognizable rumbling sound overhead erased the last bits of confusion. She had fallen through the basement floor of the Timberton Hotel. But, into what?

Paige lowered the flashlight and explored her surroundings more closely. On two sides, dirt walls faced each other, with eight to ten feet between them. The two opposing directions were open. A ditch, Paige thought. She had fallen into some type of old drainage ditch that ran below the hotel. Somewhat calmed by the knowledge that she was not enclosed in an eight by eight foot space, she struggled to her feet. Aside from the gash on her head, the throbbing headache, muscle pains and bruises from the fall and having no conceivable reason whatsoever for having been in the cellar to begin with, her situation wasn't all that bad, was it? After a hot bath, some painkillers and a cold compress across her forehead, she might even be able to think up a way to explain it all to Betty.

Paige reached for the closest wall and leaned against it for support. Expecting the texture of dirt or mud, she was surprised to find a rough, scratchy surface. She swung the flashlight around quickly. The light revealed a timber beam, securely wedged inside the packed dirt and another, just like it, a few feet away. She moved forward, stepping around the scattered debris. Yet another beam came into view, this one attached to a crossbeam above.

The ceiling was barely a foot above her head. She was no longer standing under the hotel's flimsy basement. Lifelong claustrophobic tendencies aside, she was now growing concerned. Why would a ditch have such a carefully constructed interior? Unless.... Paige aimed the light at the ground and scuffed the surface with one shoe, brushing dirt clods and gravel aside. A glimmer of metal appeared. As she continued to clear the floor, the dull, scratched surface of a rail became visible. She had fallen into an old mining tunnel.

Despite a rising panic and a pounding headache that was growing worse by the minute, Paige couldn't help feeling she might have accidentally kicked the article for *The Manhattan Post* up a few notches. After all, she'd fallen into good stories before, though not literally. If she could tie in the tunnel discovery with Timberton's sapphire mining history, she'd have an exceptional piece. That is, once she got out of her current predicament.

Paige returned to the spot where she'd originally landed and looked up into the hotel's basement, turning the flashlight off to save the battery. The distance she'd fallen was no more than twelve feet. Given a tall ladder she might have been able to climb out. But with nothing to stand on, her five-foot plus height wasn't going to get her anywhere. She had to find another way out.

In the dim light, Paige assessed the tunnel's directions. Surely there was an opening at one end. Mist had described Hollister's compartment under the trestle. Could the tunnel's entrance be there? It was her best hunch.

Visualizing the layout of the town, Paige figured the Timberton Trestle was no more than a half mile away to her left. Or was it to her right? She looked up into the gaping hole above her again and gathered her bearings. Left, definitely left. Clicking the flashlight back on, she started in that direction.

Whatever panic Paige had managed to avoid so far came rushing at her twenty yards later. The light from the basement had been more useful than she had realized. As soon as it faded behind her, the flashlight's beam became nothing but a small blur. She pictured the buildings above ground as she moved forward – the candy store, the saloon, the gem gallery. But her imagination was no match for the oppressive darkness. She fought back tears as she followed the tiny light in front of her feet. She could almost hear her grandmother reproaching her with one of her standard clichés: "Curiosity killed the cat." This had to be the worst situation Paige's curiosity had ever gotten her into.

Progress through the tunnel was slow. Paige took small, cautious steps to avoid stumbling. She fought to control her breathing, to keep her fear from causing her to hyperventilate. What structures were above each section of the tunnel? If the floor beneath the hotel was unstable, what was to say the same wasn't true of other places along the tunnel's route?

Some self-preservation instinct made her raise her free hand toward the tunnel ceiling as she moved forward, just in time to keep her head from smacking against a low crossbeam. She touched her forehead just below the wound.

A sudden clanking echo from behind her sent her into a panic. She held her breath, listening for movement, then exhaled. It was yet another of the hotel boiler's outbursts. She continued to make her way through the tunnel.

She aimed the flashlight at her watch to see that it had taken the better part of an hour for her to reach the part of the tunnel nearest the trestle. She had managed to stay calm by reminding herself that each step brought her closer to the end. The longer she walked, the sooner she'd be out. Those hopes came to an abrupt halt when she reached her intended destination. Instead of an exit there was only a wall.

Frantically, she moved from one side of the tunnel to the other, certain there was a way through. Yet she found nothing but a solid surface. Had she chosen the wrong direction? It didn't matter. Either way, she'd come to a dead end.

Paige retraced her steps, arriving once again below the hotel's crumbled basement floor. Swallowing her pride, she shouted for help and waited for a response. When none came, she yelled a second time and a third, pausing between shouts when the belching of the boiler drowned out her cries. Exhausted from the physical ordeal and emotional stress, Paige found the thought of sitting down to rest almost irresistible. Someone was sure to find her. But what if no one noticed her missing until the next day? The thought of spending the night alone in the tunnel terrified her. She had to find a way out.

If the first route she had taken was the dead end it appeared to be, the exit had to be in the opposite direction. Yet again she looked up into the hotel basement and cried for help, but it was clear that no one could hear her. Betty and Mist weren't likely to be back until later. There was no way she was willing to wait hours for them to return. The only reasonable option was to follow the tunnel to the opposite end and find the exit.

Paige was relieved to find the second route straighter than the other, allowing her to cover more ground before losing the light from the basement. She kept the flashlight turned off until it became absolutely necessary to have it on. Once the light behind her faded into black, she clicked on the dim light, willing it to last until she reached the tunnel's exit. Aiming it alternately at the floor and the ceiling, she sidestepped rocks that might trip her, as well as crossbeams that could break her head wound open. Continued outbursts from the boiler caused her to jump a few times.

Just a little farther, she told herself. She forced herself to take one exhausted step after another.

Noticing the flashlight growing dimmer, she shut it off and extended both arms out in front of her. If her forward motion angled off-track, her arms would let her know she'd turned toward a wall. She could then straighten out and continue on. After she'd covered several segments this way, her arms brushed the wall. She adjusted the direction at a right angle and began to move forward, only to find herself up against the wall again. Puzzled, she assumed she had over-corrected and angled back. Still she came up against the wall. With a rising knot in her stomach, she placed her hands flat against the wall and patted her way along it, finding that it angled sharply into another wall and, after that, yet another. There was no way around it. She had come to a dead end, just as she had when she sought the exit in the opposite direction.

Tears of panic welled up. How could there be no exit? What meager amount of energy she'd had after tumbling through the basement floor was gone. She fell back against the nearest wall and slid to the ground. Hugging her knees, she let the sobs come.

CHAPTER TWENTY-SIX

Betty and Mist stumbled in the front door, Betty laughing and Mist following behind, smiling. Both held hefty boxes, two of many still left to be unloaded. They'd stocked up on every conceivable grocery item, plus numerous non-edible purchases, ranging from paper towels to cleansers. It was enough to help keep Timberton fed for a good two weeks without needing another out-of-town run.

Setting the boxes on the kitchen's center table, Mist went back to the car for another load. Betty switched the radio on, determined to continue the light mood they'd caught while running errands.

"Sometimes it takes getting out of Timberton to bring a little pizzazz back into it. Yes, it does," Betty said to herself. She turned up the radio's volume and tested out a few dance steps on her way back to the boxes.

"You love to dance," Mist observed as she returned with a box of fresh produce.

Betty hummed and nodded. She pulled a gallon jug of maple syrup out of a bag and set it down next to stacks of eggs in square trays.

"I danced when I was younger. My sister and I both did." Betty paused, remembering. "We didn't take lessons or anything like that. But my, oh my, we loved to dance. We could put on any type of music and come up with the most splendid routines."

"I didn't know you had a sister." Mist's voice was soft against the bold volume of the radio, but Betty either heard her or knew instinctively what she would say.

"Her name was Abby. She's passed on – cancer, horrible. She was only a little older, but we got along fine, though we had our differences and could be competitive, like ordinary sisters."

"Competitive in what way?"

"Oh, you know, the usual stuff – clothes, attention, boys…" Betty's voice trailed off before picking up the beat again. "Mostly we just had fun – making up games, trying on jewelry from our mother's top dresser drawer when she wasn't looking, reading, dancing, laughing."

"I've wondered sometimes what it would have been like to have a sister. Or brother, for that matter." Mist was lining up produce, taking inventory. Potatoes to cube and roast with rosemary and garlic. Carrots to shred for fresh carrot cake. Different types of squash to steam with slices of tomato and onion.

"You're an only child?"

"Yes, raised by my grandmother after my parents were killed in a car accident when I was young."

"I'm sorry." Betty paused. "I didn't realize."

Mist smiled. "Don't be sorry. Life happens as it's supposed to."

"You really believe that, don't you?" Betty couldn't help but be envious of Mist's serene attitude toward life.

"Yes, I do." As always, Mist's voice was soothing. "We aren't always happy with what life gives us, but it's all part of a universal balance."

Betty smiled. It was so like Mist to approach life's challenges metaphysically. She finished emptying the last box, setting out large packages of dried pasta and two restaurant-sized cans of tomato sauce.

"Pasta tonight?" Mist eyed the supplies on the counter, already running a selection of spices through her head.

Betty nodded. "Yes, nice and easy. It'll feed a lot of people. Pull out one of those big pots. No, make that two - one for the pasta and one for the sauce."

Mist put out three, figuring an extra for the squash medley, as well. "We should start the sauce now. I'll add spices. It should simmer for a while. Is there bread? The bakery should still have some from this morning. I'll make garlic bread."

"Good idea," Betty said. "Go on down and see what they have. We can put the rest of the supplies away in the storage pantry later. Right now I just want to get tonight's dinner started."

"Perfect. Thanks for letting me help cook, Betty. I don't feel like myself without a kitchen."

Betty laughed. "Don't worry. Townsfolk will be chipping in when they come eat, and they'll sure chip in more if you're cooking, instead of me."

"I'll see if Paige wants to go to the bakery with me." Mist left the kitchen, headed upstairs. Betty kicked up a few more dance steps as the radio moved into Bill Haley's "Rock Around the Clock."

Mist was back quickly, sticking her head in the kitchen. "There was no answer when I knocked on her door. Maybe she's up at Clive's."

"That would be my guess," Betty agreed. "Her rental car is out in front, so she can't be far."

"I'll stop by Clive's after I pick up the bread. I want to see how he's doing, anyway." Mist disappeared from the kitchen, and Betty heard the hotel's front door shut behind her. Betty turned the radio volume up and starting slicing squash and onions.

* * * *

The frontage of the gem gallery looked almost neon in the late afternoon sun. Bright as the paint was when the sun was high above, it was just short of blinding when the rays hit it from a low angle. Inside, things were much calmer.

"No tourists today?" Mist asked, finding Clive alone at his desk. The worktables looked untouched and the floor, swept clean. Clive's gloomy expression answered her question.

"Won't be many until next spring," Clive said. "Fall never brings people in, and winter's right around the corner. Had some flurries just the other day. Summer's the only money-maker and the next one's a far stretch ahead of us."

Mist pulled a chair up next to his desk and sat. "How do you get by between summers, Clive? Seems you thrive on the activity and sales this place provides. I don't mean just financially. You seem happiest when the gallery is busy."

Clive smiled, touched by Mist's concern and impressed with her powers of perception. "I can usually make ends meet by stretching the summer earnings over the year. Lots of business owners in tourist towns get by that way. Not impossible, as long as you keep life simple. Then I have jewelry sales and rent…." He stopped short; he didn't want Mist to worry about the café not generating rent anymore. "And you're right, I like it when this place is busy. Smiling travelers, happy children and all that. Time flies by. And it keeps me from being lonely, I guess."

"I thought as much," Mist said, her voice light. "There's often something tender hidden in someone's heart when that heart is wrapped up in a gruff exterior."

"I don't know anyone with a gruff exterior," Clive said. It was more of a bark than a comment.

"Who was she?" Mist's question was posed so softly that Clive wasn't sure she'd spoken at all. He stalled before answering.

"It was a long time ago."

"Sometimes the past and the present are the same." Mist stood up and walked to the front window, looking back toward the hotel and, beyond that, the ruins of the café. "Then again, sometimes they're not."

Clive sighed, shook his head and picked up a stack of bills, shuffling through them. There were days when he was comforted by Mist's odd manner and philosophies, but this wasn't one of them. Sometimes she hit too close to home.

"How's our reporter friend doing?" Clive asked, eager to change the subject.

Mist turned back to face the gallery interior. "I saw her this morning, but not since. Betty and I made a supply run, hoping to keep this town fed for the near future, at least. I thought maybe Paige would be here. We could use help preparing dinner."

"Sorry, I haven't seen her. She must have enough information about sapphire mining, not that she ever seems to run out of questions." Clive laughed. "But the supply run sounds promising. What's on the menu for tonight?"

"Pasta," Mist answered simply before her mouth lifted into a soft upward curve. "Pasta and sunshine."

"Now you're messing with me," Clive accused.

Mist smiled. "Yes, I am. But not about the pasta. See you anytime after six."

CHAPTER TWENTY-SEVEN

Paige inhaled slowly to the count of five and exhaled in the same manner. She counted breaths until she felt her fear ease. Focused breathing always helped her fight panic attacks, and the one she was currently having felt overwhelming. She struggled to her feet and leaned against the tunnel wall for support. She groped the muddy surface to get her bearings. There had to be a way out.

Which direction led back to the hotel's basement? She clicked her flashlight on, grateful she'd saved battery life by turning it off earlier. A swing of light to her left revealed the dead end wall. The opposite direction would let her retrace her steps.

She aimed the light at the tunnel's ceiling, inspecting the crossbeams above. The thick wood was firmly embedded in the solid dirt overhead. Switching the flashlight's focus to the area around her feet, she could see the dusty traces of tracks, just as she'd seen at the opposite end of the tunnel. They ran the length of the interior, obscured by dirt that had built up over a century.

She then ran the flashlight beam over the walls, which were a solid mix of mud and timber, just like the rest. She began to make her way back toward the collapsed basement floor of the hotel. Betty and Mist would be back from their supply run by now. Surely, if she screamed loud enough, they would hear her.

She continued to shift the light as she walked. Each section of the tunnel was identical until she reached a spot approximately twenty yards from the dead end behind her. There, the texture of the wall became rough. She brushed clumps of dirt to the ground. Beneath the crusted surface, a slat of wood appeared. And then another alongside it. One by one, she uncovered additional wooden boards until she realized what she'd discovered. There was a door built into the wall. Her spirits lifted. This had to be the way out.

Attacking the surrounding area, she worked at getting the door open. Dirt wedged itself beneath her nails, rendering them as caked and dirty as the rest of her body. The thought of a hot shower flitted across her mind, another thing to anticipate once she got out. If she got out. Quickly, she discarded the last thought. This was no time for pessimism.

It was hard to tell if she was making progress, but she continued to dig. The wooden slats held their positions. She gathered her strength – what little she had – and threw one shoulder up against the wood. Still nothing. She repeated the process, alternating shoulders, then resorted to kicking the wood. When that failed, she scoured the ground and found a flat rock about the size of her fist. Using it to dig around the edge of the slats, she finally felt one move. Encouraged, she wedged the rock between that slat and the next, applying leverage until the loose one gave way. As she suspected, the area behind it was hollow. It was just what she'd hoped for. She'd found a side passage.

One by one, she pried the slats out until an opening formed that was wide enough for her to step inside. Eager to hurry toward the exit, she climbed through and took only a few steps before she bumped her already throbbing head against another barrier. She reached up to touch her forehead, but she hadn't hit it hard enough to cause more bleeding.

Regrouping, she picked up the flashlight again and aimed its beam in front of her, expecting to find another muddy wall. Instead the light landed on a row of slender packages, each an inch or two thick, approximately three feet in height, covered in butcher paper, with twine wrapped around them. They sat on a makeshift shelf, set on two barrels, which brought their top corners to Paige's own height.

Looking closer, Paige was able to make out numbers on the edge of each package, scrawled in handwriting that looked oddly familiar. Exhaustion and her aching head made it harder for her to remember where she'd seen this handwriting before. But after a minute, it came to her: the penmanship matched the writing in Silas Wheeler's diary.

As eager as she was to rip open one of the packages, she was even more anxious to get to the exit. Her body ached from bruises, cuts and exhaustion. Her ears pounded so fiercely she couldn't tell whether the sound was an underground echo or came from inside her own head. Grasping one of the butcher-papered objects, she pulled it forward and leaned it against the dirt wall to the side. Yanking another one off the shelf, she added that to the first. Slowly, she moved the packages until she'd cleared the board and was able to remove it. When she stepped between the barrels, she found herself in front of yet another makeshift shelf, also holding a row of packages. How many were there? She'd pulled at least a dozen off the first shelf and the second was even more heavily stacked.

She pushed on, her arms growing shakier with each package she moved. How long had she been trapped in the tunnel? When had she last eaten? Time had blurred. Her strength was fading.

Once she had moved and stacked the packages from the second shelf, she lifted the board, set it aside and prayed she wouldn't find yet a third shelf full of packages. To her relief, she didn't. But, ten yards or so later, she came to something worse: a solid wall. She had reached another dead end. As if that wasn't bad enough, she soon had a new problem. The flashlight flickered, dimmed, flickered again and then went out altogether.

The darkness that now surrounded Paige suffocated her. Panic filled her lungs and muddled her mind. Was there no exit at all? How would she find out without being able to see? She began to feel light-headed, and a familiar and unwelcome prickly heat ran up her arms and neck. She was on the brink of fainting. Her breathing became shallow and she dropped to the ground, hung her head forward and took slow, deep breaths. Eyes closed and neck relaxed, she focused. If she wanted to get out, she had to remain conscious and coherent.

The dizziness that had sent her to the ground began to ease. She stood up and opened her eyes even though she knew she wouldn't be able to see anything in the blackness.

She clicked the flashlight's switch again. Still dead. She would have to feel her way back through the tunnel to the section under the hotel cellar.

Testing the ground around her with one foot, she found it clear. She took one cautious step after another, checking the ground in front of her for obstacles. When she reached the wall, she placed her palms against the dirt surface and appraised her surroundings from memory. She would have to maneuver around the packages without falling. After that she could move forward.

CHAPTER TWENTY-EIGHT

Susan was hunched over paperwork, debating whether to run a story on urban renewal or recent advances in pollution deterrence, when Brandi sashayed into her office.

"The ad department says they're getting slammed with requests to run display ads in the edition that'll be out during the convention," Brandi said.

"Good, I like to hear that. When they're happy, I'm happy – mostly because they leave me alone." Susan's gaze never left the draft layouts on her desk.

"But I'm also getting calls from individual jewelers," Brandi added, looking down at the gold metallic strapped pumps she was wearing. Maybe purple lace-ups would have been a better choice for her black leather skirt. The shiny gold just didn't go with the silver studs that ran the length of the skirt's side seams.

"OK," Susan replied. Her vague tone made it clear she was paying about as much attention to the conversation as Brandi, who contemplated a shimmering toe while waiting for direction. Maybe silver flats would have been the best option.

"Brandi?" Susan coaxed her to continue. It wasn't unusual for Brandi to lose her train of thought mid-stream.

"Alan, at Al's A Gem, doesn't want to run a large ad without Yogo jewelry in stock," Brandi said. "And Simon, at Stoned in Manhattan, has a few loose Yogos in his stash, but they aren't set. So he's holding out altogether unless he can get ready-to-sell pieces in."

"Simon has a few loose screws in his stash, as well," Susan commented, without looking up. "I dare say he named his store appropriately."

Brandi watched Susan set aside one layout and pull another in front of her, unsure what her next step should be. "So, I can't get these jewelers to commit to ads when they don't already have Yogo jewelry in stock. They want international guests from the convention to buy on the spot."

"What about Sid?" Susan asked. "It was his idea to go after this article to begin with."

Brandi was glad to have an opening to pass on a piece of positive news. "No problem with Sid's Jewelers. They committed right away to a large display. It's just the others I'm having trouble with. They all want more Yogos in stock first."

"Then go find some." Susan raised her head slightly and peered over a pair of reading glasses. "If anyone can track down jewelry, Brandi, I'd think it would be you." Her glance fell on a set of rhinestone bangles that stacked up along Brandi's arm.

Brandi giggled. "A jewelry hunt! Count me in!" Her bracelets jangled as she clapped her hands.

"I knew I could count on you," Susan replied with an all-business tone. "Bring those ads in, one way or another. I want this advertising angle to work. It'll buy us new avenues for articles in future issues."

Brandi practically skipped back to her desk, diving right into her task. Maybe eBay. Maybe Amazon. She wrapped one hand around her bracelets and twisted her arm back and forth. Where would a person find jewelry, other than a jewelry store?

As if anticipating Brandi's confusion, Susan's voice suddenly soared across the office.

"Wholesalers, Brandi. Try wholesalers." A pause followed. "And check in with Paige to see how the article's progressing."

CHAPTER TWENTY-NINE

Betty had just finished drying dishes when the phone rang. The turnout for dinner had been large enough to go through ten pounds of dry pasta, two number ten cans of tomato sauce and seven loaves of bread. Mist's sourdough slices had been the hit of the evening, steaming hot and bursting with the combined flavors of butter, garlic and Parmesan cheese.

"Hello, Betty? It's Jake, Paige's friend from Jackson."

Betty rubbed both hands with a kitchen towel, phone propped between her chin and shoulder. She wasn't surprised he was calling. She'd seen the sparks between them when he came up to Timberton to surprise Paige.

"Yes, Jake. Good to hear from you." Mist popped her head into the kitchen because of the sound of the ringing phone. Betty shook her head, indicating that the phone call wasn't from Paige.

"Betty, I'm sorry to bother you, but is Paige around? I've been trying to reach her, but her cell phone keeps going to voicemail."

"I wish I could tell you she was here," Betty said. "But we haven't seen her. Mist checked down at Clive's, and I've checked the hotel messages. We thought she'd be here for dinner."

"That's odd." Jake sounded puzzled. "We had a painting checked out by an art appraiser. I heard from the guy and wanted to fill her in, but she hasn't returned my messages. She was expecting me to call."

"Jake, I don't know what to tell you. She didn't say she was going anywhere. Besides, wouldn't she have taken her car?"

"Her car is there?" Jake's tone became serious.

"Yes, right out in front of the hotel." Betty was growing more concerned as the conversation continued.

"Really, it hasn't been that long," Betty continued. "We saw her this morning before we ran out to pick up supplies. When we returned this afternoon, we figured she'd gone for a long walk, or was hiding out somewhere to write. There didn't seem to be any reason to worry."

"Did you check her room?"

"Mist knocked on her door earlier and didn't get an answer. She figured Paige was sleeping or working. Or up at Clive's, which she wasn't. But I used my master key to check inside the room when she didn't come to dinner. She's not here. Mist and Clive just went back up to his place to check there again."

"Did you call the sheriff?"

"No, not yet," Betty said. "But I'm going to now."

"I'm getting off the line so you can call him. Have him search the hotel, her room, her car, the whole town. You have my number, right?"

"Yes, from arranging the dinner at Moonglow." Betty's voice was shaky now. "I'll call you as soon as I hear anything."

As soon as she ended the call with Jake, she dialed the sheriff's number.

* * * *

It was a good half hour before Sheriff Myers pulled up in front of the hotel. He'd been halfway to Utica when Betty's call reached him. A quick U-turn sent him back toward Timberton.

Betty threw open the front door of the hotel before the sheriff was even out of his vehicle. She'd been watching out the window ever since calling him, hoping to see the patrol car arrive quickly or, better yet, to see Paige stroll up. The Timberton Hotel had never had a guest disappear, so that in itself was alarming. And she'd grown fond of Paige during her short stay.

"So, your girl's gone missing, the reporter? What was her name again?" The sheriff took his time walking up to the hotel, pulling a notepad and pen out of his front pocket along the way.

"Paige MacKenzie," Betty said quickly, leaning forward to watch the sheriff write down the name, as if seeing it in print might make the actual person appear.

"And when did you last see Ms. MacKenzie?"

"This morning. Make that late morning, right before Mist and I made a supply run." Betty wrapped her arms around her own waist, an unconscious attempt to comfort herself.

Sheriff Myers paused. "So, it hasn't been that long. Maybe she just went out for a drive."

Betty removed one arm from around her body long enough to point at the curb where the sheriff saw the rental car parked in front of the hotel. He turned back to face her.

"Well, perhaps a long walk?" The sheriff lifted his shoulders in a casual, questioning manner. "After all, it's only been a few hours."

"It has not been just a few hours, Sheriff Myers," Betty bristled. "It has been a solid ten hours. I could walk from one end of this town to the other and back twenty times in that same amount of time. Don't tell me she just went for a walk."

The sheriff sighed, lifting up the pen and paper and preparing to write again. "OK, list the places she usually goes. Maybe she's sick or injured – a sprained ankle or something. That could stop her getting back."

"She has a cell phone," Betty pointed out. "She would have called here or notified someone she knows if she couldn't get back."

"Now, you know how spotty coverage can be out here," Sheriff Myers countered.

"The gem gallery," Betty snapped.

"What?"

"Write it down," Betty said, exasperated. "You asked for places she usually goes. That's one."

"OK, where else?" The sheriff now had the list started.

Betty rubbed her forehead, thinking. "Well, I would have said Moonglow, but obviously that's not a current option. Though I wouldn't put it past her to dig through the rubble. Better take a look there."

"Got it. Other ideas?"

"Obviously her room upstairs, number sixteen, but I just checked there about an hour ago."

The sheriff nodded. "I'll check again. She might go straight back there without thinking people could be worried about her being gone. As I said, it hasn't been very long." He cleared his throat.

Betty ignored his last comment.

"You might try the park, where Hollister hangs out. She knows Mist has been helping him. She might have gone to check on him herself. You might look under the trestle, too."

"Under the Timberton Trestle?" Sheriff Myers looked up from his notepad. "Why?"

"Because that's where Hollister sleeps. Didn't you know that?" Betty looked puzzled. It seemed a sheriff should know everything about a community.

Sheriff Myers furrowed his brow and shook his head. "No, I didn't. And I've driven by that trestle plenty on regular patrols. I've never seen him there."

"Well, apparently he sleeps inside that grate, at least that's what Mist says."

"You don't say." The sheriff looked lost in thought.

"Sheriff Myers, we're not looking for Hollister at the moment," Betty said, her voice stern. "We're looking for Paige."

The sheriff scribbled a few more notes, shut his notebook and stuffed it in his pocket, along with his pen. "I'll check all those areas, including the roped-off café ruins and the grate under the trestle. Also, Clive's place and the outskirts of the town in all directions, just in case she did go out walking and got herself injured. You said her room is number sixteen?"

It did not slip past Betty that he emphasized the words "roped off" when referring to the café. Paige did seem to push the limits. But being judgmental wouldn't help find a missing person. She only nodded silently as he stepped past her and headed up the stairs.

CHAPTER THIRTY

Jake downshifted and started uphill. The ten percent grade that marked the beginning of the stretch over Teton Pass was not his favorite section of road. He preferred heading out of Jackson Hole from the north end of the valley, up through Yellowstone National Park. This time it wasn't an option. The south entrance to the park was already closed in preparation for winter. His only choice was to detour through Idaho.

The weather was clear, so he easily made it down into the flatland that backed the Tetons without any problems. After he passed through the town of Victor, he turned north. One by one, he put small Idaho towns behind him, keeping a steady foot on the accelerator. He was tempted to push the speed limit, but he knew better than to risk it. Getting pulled over in a small town in the middle of the night would cause more of a delay than taking it slow.

Had Jake not been consumed with worry, he might have tried to calm Betty down on the phone. But he only had one thing on his mind: making sure Paige was safe. Logic had told him to stay put and wait for Timberton's locals to find Paige. In view of the late night hour, the sheriff was their best hope. By the time he arrived in Timberton, it would be nearly 4 a.m. If Paige was in trouble, that could be too late. But there was little chance of sleeping when his nerves were wound tighter than a lassoed calf.

He'd managed to chug four cups of coffee while tossing a change of clothes and a toothbrush into a duffel bag. Pacing back and forth inside the ranch house would have only revved up his anxiety. If nothing else, driving would give him something to do.

For all he knew, there was no reason for worry. Paige was stubbornly independent. Her cell battery could easily have run out, in which case she wouldn't have gotten anyone's messages. She could be holed up somewhere writing, lost in thought, without any clue that people were worried about her. He had to believe this.

Temporarily reassured by these thoughts, he forced himself to view the drive as simply an excuse to spend another day with her, not the panicked trip it actually was. It would give him a chance to discuss Lambert's findings with her in person. He could hardly wait to see her face when she heard the painting was worth more than they'd originally thought.

It was fortunate Lambert had the connections he did. A call to an old colleague, an art historian at the Smithsonian, had turned up an unexpected twist – a second painting. The idea that another painting of Silas Wheeler's had come under question had never entered Lambert's mind. As it turned out, a small faction of art enthusiasts had suspected for some time that an unknown western painter had produced at least one remarkable piece of work, yet had passed it off as the work of Silas Wheeler. The question had always been why? With only one example of art by the mystery painter, there had been little reason for controversy. The painting was simply what it was – a single piece of exceptional artwork.

Until now. Now there were two, which made it an entirely different situation, according to Lambert. One painting could easily be a fluke. But the surfacing of a second meant there was a pattern. If there were two, could there be more? And just how exceptional were these paintings? Would there be a demand for them? Would they have value?

Jake passed through West Yellowstone and continued north along Hwy 191, through the Gallatin National Forest. The spectacular scenery along this stretch of highway made it a favorite drive of his during daylight hours. Now, at midnight, it was just another lonely highway. He leaned forward, adjusted his seating position, shrugged his shoulders up and down to release tension and settled back again in the truck's seat.

Jake had heard the excitement in Lambert's voice as he shared the new information about the paintings. Although he appreciated a nice piece of western art, Jake had never been much of a painting connoisseur. Still, he could understand how the discovery of an unknown painter would be news in the art world. Had Paige stumbled onto something much bigger than she thought?

He cruised into Bozeman just before midnight, stopping only long enough to gas up the truck and try to call Paige. Still no answer. He bought a cup of coffee and a bag of chips from a convenience store on the edge of town and got right back on the road. If he kept making good time, he could be in Timberton between 3 and 4 a.m. By then, Paige would be safe, sound and asleep in her room at the hotel, cell phone plugged into its charger. Yes, he was certain that would be the case.

Just over three hours later, Jake pulled up in front of the Timberton Hotel. The front porch light was on, along with the lobby lights. Jake threw on the emergency brake, hopped out of the truck and approached the entrance. Not bothering to ring the bell, he twisted the doorknob, found it unlocked and shoved it open. Jake made a beeline for the second floor, taking the stairs two at a time. He arrived at Paige's room to find the door open, lights on and no sign of Paige anywhere.

It was clear the room had been searched thoroughly. Dresser drawers stood ajar, as did both doors to the room's walnut wardrobe. The contents of Paige's briefcase were spread across the bed's quilted duvet, spiral notepads left open and manila file folders strewn against the pillows, her cell phone alongside. Sweaters and T-shirts spilled over the edge of her luggage, including a draped sliver of black lace. Jake felt a protective surge of discomfort at the thought of the sheriff rummaging through Paige's intimate apparel.

"Jake, is that you?" Betty's voice called up from below.

"Yes!" Jake shouted, doubling back down the stairs. He half hoped to find Paige, Mist and Betty sitting together in the kitchen, sipping hot chocolate and laughing about the false alarm. Instead, he found Betty twisting her hands in a peach floral apron. Her normally coiffed hair was disheveled, her face drawn from lack of sleep. Jake's fears multiplied instantly.

"No sign of her? Nothing?" Jake heard the fear in his own voice. Betty shook her head.

"Sheriff Myers has been here three times, each time without any news, just asking questions and going through Paige's room over and over."

Jake took Betty's arm and led her to a lobby chair, easing her into it. "I tried to call you again after I left Bozeman, but couldn't get decent cell reception."

Betty tried to stand back up immediately, but Jake encouraged her to rest. "Let the sheriff do his job, Betty. If you can stay calm, it will help us all."

Mist brought a gust of wind into the lobby with her when she entered. She looked concerned, but composed, as usual. She said a quick hello to Jake then set a hand on Betty's shoulder.

"He's right, Betty. Being upset won't help us find her any faster. We'll all just end up feeding off each other's nerves. If we stay calm, we can think more clearly. Maybe we've overlooked something that will come to us if we pause long enough to let it."

"How can I just sit and relax when Paige is missing?" Betty remained seated but looked back and forth between Jake and Mist, as if together, they might have an answer as to where Paige was and why she was missing.

Jake was glad to turn the handling of Betty's nerves over to Mist. It was one thing to try to calm Betty, but another to calm himself. Sitting still was the last thing he needed. It would only make him more nervous.

"I'm going back up to Paige's room again to look for more clues. The sheriff could have missed something, even after all those searches." Jake headed for the stairs.

Mist looked up. "Sheriff Myers has been over at the gem gallery, too, asking to look through paperwork from Moonglow. I gave him the sketches. He thought they might help."

"No offense, Mist, but how could your sketches help find her? I don't get the connection." Jake paused, his foot on the first step.

"Not my own sketches," Mist said. "The sketches I found in the back of the café when I moved in. I told everyone about them the morning after the fire."

"Why would the sheriff be looking through papers at the gem gallery?" Jake said. "He should be out physically searching the area."

Mist moved her shoulders to indicate a shrug, but in such a way that it resembled more of a ballet move. Jake doubted he'd ever become used to her unearthly behavior.

"He is out searching the area, Jake," Betty said. "And he's been checking in here. I think he's just trying to be thorough."

"I suppose so," Jake said, though he looked unconvinced. He sprinted up the stairs. There had to be something everyone else was missing.

CHAPTER THIRTY-ONE

Sheriff Myers sat in his parked patrol car a few miles outside of town. It was a lucky break, having that New York reporter go missing. He hadn't counted on such a stroke of good fortune. For all the times he'd tried to come up with plausible excuses to search Timberton's Main Street buildings, this excuse was the best. No one would be suspicious now. He could snoop around all he wanted. After all, he was just doing his job.

Each search inside a town building gave him a chance to collect information. Each trip outside the town limits allowed time to inspect and analyze anything he'd found. The reporter had left a hefty stash of notes on local sapphire mining, far more information than he'd accumulated himself. He'd found the expected paraphernalia of a woman traveler – clothing, toiletries and make-up – as well as a tattered, old journal in her room, but he'd left all that behind. He wasn't interested in the woman's personal belongings and some old man's stupid ramblings about artwork. Those wouldn't help him find what he was looking for. He did take one of her sweaters, just to make his search look legit. But the sapphire mining history notes could come in handy. Even better, the sketches he'd conned out of that hippie chick could be valuable.

It hadn't been his plan to come out west, but cousin Sid had been all revved up. With a change of wardrobe, a scruffy beard and a cowboy hat, Myers could blend into the western scenery, Sid had insisted. All he had to do was keep his mouth shut and limit his responses to a few words, like "Yes, Ma'am," "Nope" and "Thank you." There was no way his thick New Jersey accent would be obvious if he didn't blast his mouth off. Just to make sure, he'd practiced a western drawl. A few late nights with John Wayne helped do the trick. Hell, it wasn't that hard. After all, he'd been an acting student long before choosing a more profitable career as a thief and con man.

He spread out one of the sketches on the seat of the patrol car and switched on the overhead light. A rough square with vertical lines was all that was on the paper. It probably represented something, but wasn't enough to mean anything on its own. One by one, he spread out sheets and set them aside, finally coming to one that held his interest. The drawing showed squares and rectangles on the right half of the page, many in a row. Long lines ran along the center of the sheet, starting at the top and curving off to the right at the bottom. Fainter, dotted lines ran along the right margin, overlapping at times with the square and rectangular shapes.

He squinted at the paper, moving it around under the patrol car's light, inspecting it from different angles until he recognized the drawing was an outline of Timberton. The long lines referred to the main street, while the various box shapes represented buildings. And the dotted lines...bingo. It hit him like a bolt of lightning. Exactly as he'd hoped to find, those had to mark old mining tunnels. Sid had been right. The reporter was going to lead them to sapphires and then lead them right back to immediate sales. They'd be ready when all those international buyers came through the city with their bank rolls. And, with the amount he'd siphon off behind Sid's back, he'd be ready to retire. A modest villa along the French Riviera sounded especially enticing.

It was an easy, quick scheme: Follow the reporter to the town, then to the gem gallery, then to the source of the gallery's goods, then back to Sid's place, where they'd turn it all over quickly. She'd do the legwork, and they'd lap up the rewards. Now the only challenge that remained was to find the sapphires and get out of Timberton before anyone became suspicious. As much as that New York troublemaker had been butting her nose into people's business all over town, it would spell bad news if she got interested in what he was doing. That could be messy. He'd have all the hassle of covering tracks. No, keeping it simple was key.

He inspected the map more carefully. Even as sure as he was that the dotted lines represented a tunnel, there was no indication of a way to get inside. Old mining tunnels ran through many parts of the area, but entrances had long since been boarded up or filled in, for safety. When the café burned down, he'd hoped the cellar would have a trap door to a tunnel. No such luck.

It was the same with other basements around town, at least those he'd been able to inspect. He'd just about run out of creative excuses to gain access. The candy store had been easy, what with the owner always thinking the register was short. He'd browsed around inside that store plenty of times. The saloon, too, had been easy. The night bartender packed away so much whiskey he'd never notice customers dancing on the bar counter, much less anyone casually poking around walls and floors. And any decent sheriff would keep an eye on a homeless man, so it had been a cinch to check every inch of the park, even with that weirdo café chick hanging around a lot to keep the old guy company. If there were any entrances within the town itself, he hadn't been able to find them.

Frustrated, he stepped out of the car, shuffled his boots around in the roadside dirt and kicked the front tire of the vehicle. He looked down at the boots with disgust. How did these western cowboys manage to wear them, anyway? He supposed they might feel different once they were broken in, but these brand spankin' new buckets of stiff leather had him yearning for his soft, Italian loafers. He could hardly wait to get back to the East Coast and leave this costume gig behind.

Which reminded him, time was running short. Sid had made it clear he needed to get into town, find a stash of sapphires and get back out before anyone became suspicious or, worse yet, found the real Sheriff Myers where he'd left him. Not to mention the fact that the gem conference was coming up fast. Sid needed time to set the stones. And options were limited for handling stolen jewels. There weren't many trustworthy crooks. He laughed out loud at the last thought. He should know.

He leaned back against the side of the patrol car and drew a pack of cigarettes from his vest. Pulling one out of the crumpled cellophane wrapper, he pressed it between his lips and lit it, cupping one hand around the tip to shield it from the wind. He inhaled and exhaled quickly, determined to figure things out. There had to be a way to get into the tunnel. If not inside the town, then where? Suddenly a smile curved up around the burning tobacco. Of course. He took one more drag, tossed the cigarette butt on the ground and smashed it flat with his boot. He jumped back into the car, fired up the ignition and drove back toward Timberton.

* * * *

Myers parked the patrol car in front of the cabin he'd been using as a temporary place to hole up. The weathered building had been the perfect spot for his makeshift living quarters. It was far enough out of Timberton and far enough from Utica to avoid attention. And its tool shed held every piece of equipment known to man and miner. Much of it was about to come in handy.

Thirty minutes later, he pulled into Timberton. The town was dark except for bright lights flowing from the hotel. Of course, that was where townsfolk would be gathering. He imagined the crowd growing as the news spread that the reporter was missing. They'd be sitting or pacing, drinking coffee and waiting for word from his latest updates on the search. As if he cared what happened to her. At least the drama was distracting the town's inhabitants.

He turned right just after passing the gem gallery, shut off the car's headlights, killed the engine and coasted down to the Timberton Trestle. Gravel popped beneath the tires as he edged the car under the pilings and stopped it. He'd packed most of the tools he needed in the trunk – a pick ax, lantern, flares, backpack, flashlight and ladder. He'd also piled the stretch of rope on the front seat, along with a tire iron and roll of duct tape. Betty had inadvertently warned him that he may have company. He'd barely opened the car door when he saw the grate swing forward. Hollister stepped out, a baffled, innocent look on his face that irritated Myers. How he hated the dumb guy's stupid expressions.

Myers put on the pretense of a smile for no more than ten seconds, the exact amount of time it took him to step casually from the car, tire iron hidden behind his back. Five seconds later, a quick blow to the side of the homeless man's head sent Hollister reeling to the ground. Myers dropped the metal tool and retrieved the rope from the car's front seat.

Dragging the unconscious man to the grate, he tied his ankles and wrists together and then wound the rope in and out of the metal design. For good measure, he wrapped duct tape around the bindings and, though it hardly seemed necessary, plastered a thick strip across Hollister's mouth.

There were definite advantages to subduing a man who couldn't talk or scream. He rarely had that luxury back east. Most guys were cursing him out before they even knew he was about to take them down. This was tidy. No sound to attract any attention. It almost took the fun out it. But it didn't matter. He had work to do.

He opened the trunk and pulled out the lantern, placing it inside the compartment behind the grate. Blankets lay tossed on the left side of the space; piles of old clothing littered the floor to the right. The back wall appeared solid, but, thanks to the sketches Mist had given him, he knew better. At least he hoped he did.

The lantern cast a low light, illuminating the floor. Myers lifted it up to bring the glow higher, taking a good look at the wall's surface. It was covered with indentations that looked like hand and fist prints, as well as scratches and scrapes that appeared to have been made by rocks or sticks. Had the town's homeless resident been trying to get through the wall, too? Did he know about the mining tunnel?

Back at the car, he lifted the pick ax out of the trunk and returned to the wall. Letting the tool hang at his side, he felt around the edges of the dirt, searching for cracks or crevices. Not finding any, he stood back, swung the pick ax over his shoulder and plunged it into the dirt. Only a few small clods fell to the ground. He attacked the surface again, with the same result. He paused and sighed. He had a feeling it was going to be a long night.

CHAPTER THIRTY-TWO

Jake returned to Paige's room to search again, no longer worried about trespassing into her private territory. His only goal was to turn up clues that could help find her. Still, even focused as he was, he lost a good three seconds when he pulled a minuscule bikini top from her suitcase. Holding onto a thin spaghetti strap, he watched it dangle in front of his face, twirling below his fingertips. He could envision the snug fit of the soft, emerald green Lycra against her smooth skin.

He dropped the skimpy top and forced himself to stick to the task. The sheriff had to have missed something. Timberton wasn't a big enough town for someone to get lost. It was a tiny, crime-free community. And Jake refused to contemplate the possibility that Paige could have come to harm.

Pushing the clothing off to the side, Jake started digging through the pockets of the suitcase. It was remarkable how complex modern luggage had become. The suitcase he'd used when he was young for family trips had been nothing more than a rectangular box with an elastic-edged pouch against the inside back panel. It had clicked shut with a flat metal latch and opened when the sides of the lock were pressed. In contrast, the piece of luggage that sat before him now might as well have been an astronaut's suit. How many zippers and compartments did the thing have, anyway? Twenty? Thirty? One after another he unzipped each section, finding only shampoo, perfume, ponytail holders, a sewing kit and granola bars, nothing that would help him find Paige. Frustrated, he abandoned the suitcase and looked around the room.

The open dresser drawers were empty, reminding him that she wasn't staying long. That thought alone sent his spirits spiraling further downward, if that was possible. The only other obvious place to search was the writing desk, where notes and folders cascaded over the edges. A tornado could not have done a better job sending them flying than the shuffling that the sheriff had obviously done. Jake gathered a handful of scattered papers from the floor and threw them on top of the desk. He lifted up an overturned chair and sat, gathering the papers in front of him. Strange how violent the sheriff had been when he searched.

Most of the paperwork was what he expected – maps of the area and outlines for the article Paige was writing. There were photographs of different stages of gem processing, ranging from the rough stone brought up from the mines right up to the polished cut gem. The examples of dazzling, finished products were numerous and varied, far more so than he'd ever considered. His impressions of precious gems had always fallen into two categories: round and not-round. But the photos Paige had gathered told a different story, one that could keep a wealthy jewelry addict busy collecting for decades. Just the variety of gem stone cuts alone was an eye-opener – emerald, princess, pear, baguette, marquise, trillion, radiant, triangle, checkerboard and briolette. The list went on and on.

Jake set the photos and outline aside. He picked up a folder with "sapphire mining history" written on the front, flipped it open but found it empty. Maybe these pages were lost somewhere in the mess on Paige's floor. Maybe the sheriff had taken the notes. There was no reason to think her disappearance had anything to do with the article. The outline was straightforward and obviously well researched. With the quantity of information Paige had accumulated during her short stay, he was surprised she wasn't already on her way back to New York. Certainly she had enough for a newspaper article.

He indulged in a bit of male ego when he hoped part of her reason for lingering was to spend time with him. But, again, that had nothing to do with why she'd be missing. It had to be a result of the one trait that often got Paige into predicaments – curiosity. And what she'd been most curious about recently was Silas Wheeler's painting.

Jake stood up, rummaged quickly through the desk drawers and slammed them shut. He scanned the room's furniture and decorative items until he saw the radiator. This triggered a memory of the first conversation he'd had with Paige about Wheeler's diary. He rushed across the room, ran his hand down the wall behind the heating unit, found the loose panel of wallboard and cast it aside. He searched the hole inside the wall. Nothing was there. Only after flattening himself on the floor and looking under the bed did he find the old diary. Myers must have tossed it there during one of his hasty searches. Jake retrieved it, sat down and scanned the entries. They were all familiar from discussions with Paige.

Finding the diary would have been encouraging had it not been for an uneasy feeling developing in his gut. Why was the diary even there? Wouldn't the sheriff have thought it interesting enough to take with him? It was an obvious lead to follow. Something wasn't right.

Jake rushed back down the stairs, where he found Betty pacing and looking out the front window. Mist sat quietly in a lobby chair, arms extended, palms up, eyes closed. Betty faced him immediately as he stepped off the last few stairs. Mist remained immobile. Jake did a double take at Mist before focusing on Betty.

"Betty, do you know anything about that old diary Paige found?" Jake asked. "Why would the sheriff leave it behind?"

Betty looked puzzled. "What old diary?"

"The one Paige found in the wall. She pulled it out, but part of it tore off and fell back inside. She's been trying to find the rest of it the whole time she's been here. She didn't mention it to you?"

"I thought she was researching sapphire mining," Betty said. "I don't know anything about a diary." She paused as Jake's words sank in. "And what do you mean she found it in the wall?"

Mist had opened her eyes and watched Betty and Jake as they exchanged questions.

"Yes, she *is* researching sapphire mining for the article," Jake said. "But she accidentally found an old diary inside the wall one night when she tried to figure out how to turn on the radiator."

Jake ran a hand through his hair. Betty was too confused to respond.

"Anyway, she thinks it was written by the artist who painted the piece in Clive's gallery. And Clive wants to sell that painting to raise money to rebuild the café. So, Paige has been trying to find the rest of it."

"I have the rest of it," Mist said. "I found it in the laundry room where the wallboard was crumbling behind the dryer."

Jake stared at Mist. "In the laundry room?"

"Yes. I wonder ... Paige came in there looking for something. I thought she wanted towels. It must have been the diary. Do you need it?" Mist stood, ready to fetch the diary remnant.

Jake shook his head. "No, I don't think the diary itself has anything to do with finding her, especially not a section she hasn't seen. The thing that hits me as strange is that the portion she found is still in her room. I don't understand why the sheriff wouldn't have taken that with him. It looks like he took the notes on sapphire mining, but nothing else. Not even her cell phone."

Now Jake was pacing. "If you were trying to find a person, wouldn't you take anything that might be a clue?" He stopped and looked at Betty and Mist

Betty was starting to see a bigger picture. "So Paige found a partial diary and was still searching for the missing part, hoping it would help Clive sell the painting to rebuild Moonglow? Is that what you're saying?"

Jake nodded. "Yes! So the question is where would she look?"

It was Mist who put the pieces together. "She didn't know I found the rest of the diary in the laundry room, so she would have kept looking for it. If she thought it had continued to fall, she would have tried another floor down."

Mist stood up and looked at Betty. "Does the hotel have a basement?"

Betty gasped. "A basement? No, that's not possible! I mean, yes, we have a basement. But we don't use it because of water damage from that old boiler. The flooring isn't safe. I keep it locked for just that reason." Betty grew more frantic with every word. "She wouldn't be able to get in there. For one thing, she wouldn't know where to find the key."

Jake closed his eyes and took a deep breath, then opened them again. "You don't know Paige. I've never met anyone as persistent in my life. If she was trying to get into the basement, she got in." He leveled his gaze on Betty. "Where do you keep the key?"

Betty spun around and bolted for the kitchen with Jake and Mist close behind. She stopped when she saw all the supply boxes stacked up on the counter, paused and patted her hands against her cheeks, as if that would help her find the key. Each time she pressed her hands to her face, her cheeks puffed out like the underbelly of a frog. The gesture reminded Jake of the fish faces kids used to make in his elementary school.

"Betty?" Jake's voice focused the hotelkeeper. She stepped forward to the sink, slid a box of groceries aside and eyed the hook where she kept keys. It was empty.

"Just as I thought," Jake said. His tone was clipped. "Where's the door to the cellar?"

Betty did a quick about face. "Follow me." Jake and Mist followed her down the main hallway to the rear of the building. The door to the cellar stood ajar, the jumbled keys hanging in the lock.

"Why wouldn't Sheriff Myers have said anything about this?" Betty said.

Jake didn't hesitate to answer. "Because he never bothered to look back here."

"But he kept coming back to search the hotel!" Betty insisted.

"I'm sure he did," Jake answered. "But he wasn't looking for Paige. He was just looking through her things." His voice trailed off as he swung the door open and started down the stairs.

"Now I'm really mixed up," Betty said.

Mist, too, looked bewildered.

CHAPTER THIRTY-THREE

Paige moved sideways, keeping both hands pressed against the tunnel's wall. Her stomach growled from hunger, and her head pounded from exhaustion and worry. The gash on her forehead stung like a family of wasps had used it as target practice. She was growing cold and starting to shiver. How many hours had she been trapped underground? Six? Eight? Twelve? If only she had her cell phone on her. It was stupid leaving it in her room, but she hadn't planned on the extended trip she was taking. Would she even be in her current predicament if she had her phone? Probably not. Cell phone reception was fine in the hotel. One quick call could've had her out hours ago.

Her balance faltered as she reached the main tunnel. She'd been leaning against the wall with increasing weight and hadn't anticipated the end of the side passage. She reassessed her direction, determining the hotel was to her left. Rounding the corner, she continued, stopping every few feet to gather strength. It was becoming more difficult to get started again each time she took a break. Her legs trembled, and her mind was foggy. Beneath all these challenges, an inner voice pushed her forward.

She'd left the packages behind, unopened, although she suspected their contents. Aside from having no light, there

was no reason to tackle them immediately. If she got out alive
– *was she really thinking 'if'* – she'd be able to check them out
later. If she didn't make it out – *was that dreadful thought even
a possibility?* – it wouldn't matter if the packages contained
mediocre paintings by Silas Wheeler or masterpieces by
Renoir.

Minutes passed, or were they hours? Her arms grew too
heavy to hold up. She resorted to leaning against the wall, her
cheek scraping against the dirt as she pushed forward. Her
legs were numb. She inched ahead, shuffling clumsily.

Eventually, she paused and let her eyelids flicker open.
Was she imagining it or was there a trace of light ahead? She
tried to calculate the distance she'd covered. Her skin was raw
from sliding against the tunnel's wall, and her mind had
grown increasingly clouded. But it seemed the reasonable
conclusion – she was nearing the section below the hotel.

Encouraged, she pried herself off the wall and took an
eager step forward, only to see the glow shift upward as her
foot caught on debris and sent her tumbling to the ground.
Her head struck a jagged rock, and the light faded away
altogether as she lapsed into unconsciousness.

CHAPTER THIRTY-FOUR

Myers leveled blows against the hard surface, watching as the mound of dirt at the base of the wall grew. Beneath his uniform, sweat poured down his back. Even the cold night air was no match for the exertion required to dig into the tunnel. He'd tossed his jacket aside not long after taking the first few swings with the pick ax.

There was no turning back now that he had the old homeless guy tied up. He'd already wasted the better part of a week trying to find the gallery's sapphire source. He was running out of time. Any day now a police supervisor could show up in town to check on the real Sheriff Myers. He needed to be long gone by then.

Irritated, he directed his frustration into attacking the wall. Sid's plan had gotten a lot more complicated than it was supposed to be. Now he had the old man to deal with and, on top of that, was supposed to be finding the reporter. Even though her disappearance had given him an excuse to search the area for the sapphires, the townsfolk still expected him to show up with her safe and sound at some point. Her nosy nature might have made her suspicious of him already. They hadn't hit it off too well the night of the fire. That could mean another messy situation he'd have to deal with.

He dropped the pick ax on the ground and glared at Hollister, who had regained consciousness. It made him nervous to have the old guy watching, even though he knew the man couldn't talk. Facing the wall again, he raised his boot and kicked the deepest section he'd dug out. Feeling the surface give a little, he kicked it again. After several tries, his foot plunged through the dirt; he'd broken into the tunnel. Maybe these boots were useful after all.

He retrieved the backpack from the car, stuck his arms through the straps and let it settle against his shoulders. He checked the ropes around Hollister's ankles and wrists to make sure they were secure. He widened the opening in the wall with the ax, then, lantern in hand, stepped inside.

The glow of the lantern was enough to light the interior. He could make out the wooden braces and crossbeams around him. But the light, which maintained a steady eight feet of illumination in front of him as he walked, couldn't define the length of the tunnel. He continued forward another fifty feet before stopping and setting the lantern down. He removed his backpack and dropped it on the ground, sitting next to it. Pulling out the papers that he'd confiscated from the weird café owner, he laid out the sketch of the tunnel layout, scooting the lantern closer to get a good look. He glanced back in the direction he'd come from and adjusted the sketch accordingly. By his calculations, he was still on the outskirts of town. He would start meandering beneath Main Street's shops another two hundred feet later.

He gulped some water from his bottle. Breaking into the tunnel had drained his energy; he was thirsty, hungry and tired. The sooner he found the gems, the sooner he could get out. He'd make sure that reporter didn't suspect anything, and then he'd pack up and split. He stood, slung his backpack over his shoulder, stuck the sketch in his front shirt pocket and proceeded on, lantern in hand.

The ground was even, aside from two rails that ran down the middle. Those were easy enough to avoid. He stepped around the metal tracks and continued another hundred yards, until a faint glow appeared ahead. For the first time, the thought occurred to him that he might not be alone. Was that possible? He'd scoured every inch of the town without finding any entrances. Only as he drew closer did the overhead light begin to make sense. It was coming from a hole in the tunnel's ceiling.

He held the lantern out as he moved ahead. The ground was covered with timber and mud. The light came from above the debris. A storage area? A basement? It didn't matter, as long as no one was there to notice him. He picked up a rock and threw it up into the room, listening for a reaction. Nothing. Assured he was alone, he stepped over the pile of rubble and kept going. Another hundred yards. And then another, until he suddenly froze. There, in the edge of the lantern's glow, was the New York reporter, collapsed on the ground.

A grin spread across his face. This was going to be easier than he thought.

Myers edged toward the reporter's motionless figure. He reached for his backpack, thinking it might be smart to pull out the knife he'd packed. But he changed his mind quickly. If a confrontation occurred, a stab wound would be too suspicious. Besides, with each step closer, it became clearer she was unconscious. If she came to, her slender frame would be no match for his brawny build, especially in the state she was in. The light from his lantern was bright enough to illuminate the gash in her forehead and residual thick, red trail of blood. She'd never have the strength to fight him.

He stepped over her. What a pain she'd been! Every time he'd come close to finding a lead on the sapphires, she'd popped up, hanging around the gem gallery or blabbing her mouth away with that wacko from California. And the way she was obviously enamored with the Wild West thing? That itself was enough to make him sick. She was a New York girl! It was downright disrespectful for her to behave like a schoolgirl at Disneyland in the dusty, rundown town of Timberton, out in the middle of nowhere. Where was her sense of East Coast pride?

On the other hand, her snoopy nature had been an asset. It hadn't been difficult to find excuses to follow her around. Meals at Moonglow had been an easy cover. Everyone needed to eat. All it had taken was a newspaper, a cup of coffee and one of the café's Strawberry-Grand Marnier tarts to give him an excuse to eavesdrop on her and that cowboy of hers. Now that he thought about it, he missed those desserts. Maybe burning down the café had been overkill, though doing so had made it easy for him to search the cellar. Waste of the old wooden shack, he supposed, considering he hadn't found anything. Historical building and all that crap.

Now the broad had served her purpose. However she'd managed to do it, she'd gotten into the tunnel and saved him a heck of a lot of searching. The side passageway she'd discovered was the perfect place for hidden gems.

After a few more steps, his lantern's glow confirmed that thought as it revealed a series of packages stacked against each wall.

He set the lantern down and studied the shape of the packages, which were numbered and wrapped in twine. They were flat, wide and rectangular, not at all what he expected. Anxious, he pulled out his knife, sliced through the twine and ripped one open, only to feel fury rising at the sight of a painting. He moved forward from one package to the next, tearing them open as he went until he gave up. Ridiculous! All this for a stack of stupid paintings? No, there had to be more. Stack by stack, he flipped through the packages. It was like being in a damn art gallery, but without wine, cheese and crackers to ease the torture of boredom. He ignored two more stacks, clearly more of the same. Frustrated, he sent one of the packages flying against the wall. It crashed with force, sending an echo back through the tunnel. He paused until silence returned, replaced the knife in his backpack and prepared to retrace his steps. He still had that idiot from the town park to deal with before he could leave.

Only as he was turning back, cursing at the time he had wasted, did he see the bundle of cloth, tucked beneath one of the stacks of packages. His heart lifted up into his throat. Of course! The paintings were just worthless diversions, meant to hide the stash with the real value. Sid had been right all along! Now he just had to get back to his cabin outside of town, portion off a good quantity for himself, and then get the heck out of Timberton. He'd be back in New York in no time, handing over what Sid thought to be the entire stash. And it would be a good three-fourths of it, or at least two-thirds. After all, there was no point in being greedy. Well, maybe half, now that he was thinking about it.

He shook the sack. It was heavy and packed solid. Excellent! That villa on the French Riviera was getting closer every minute. Tempted to break the package open and admire the haul, common sense told him the faster he got out, the better. Every second he stalled could make the difference between getting away or landing in the sheriff's office – and not in uniform, either.

He tucked the cloth bundle under his arm and was checking to make sure his hold on it was secure when he heard a soft shuffle. Had he hit something with his foot? He remained still. Was it possible, after all this, that someone had followed him? He stepped silently past the remaining packages and looked into the circle of light from the lantern. He was both relieved and disturbed to see the source of the sound was the reporter's foot scraping against the dirt. She was beginning to regain consciousness. Just what he didn't need. It wouldn't have been a problem had her eyes not opened as he stepped around her. But once they made eye contact, he knew she could have recognized him. He couldn't take that chance.

Quickly, he reached out and grasped the large rock beside her head. It was a perfect set-up, taking her out with a weapon that was already covered in her blood. Nothing could look more like an accident. He clutched the sack against his left side tightly and raised the stone overhead with his right arm. A few more seconds and the nosy snoop would no longer be a problem.

* * * *

The harsh blow struck so immediately and so unexpectedly that Myers never saw it coming. Had he not been focused on aiming for the exact location of Paige's forehead gash, he might have seen Jake's shadow just around the corner of the bend in the passageway. As it was, the only split-second warning he had was a stiff boot kick to his arm that knocked the rock he held off to the side. After that, there was only searing pain across the back of his skull. He was out cold before he hit the ground.

Jake gave Myers a vicious kick, to make sure he was unconscious. He then turned to Paige, whose eyes were half-mast as she tried to move her head and determine her whereabouts.

"Don't move," Jake ordered. He ripped off his soft red and gray shirt and pressed it against the wound on Paige's forehead. She winced as he applied pressure. "Just hang on – help will be here in a few minutes."

"Jake? What are you doing here? What happened?" she mumbled. Eyes closed again, she lifted one hand in an attempt to touch Jake's chest. Lacking strength, she let it drop.

Jake caressed her arm, found her hand and wrapped his fingers around hers. Her skin was covered with scratches and caked with mud. "I don't know the details, but it seems you fell through the cellar floor of the hotel. We'll figure it out when we get you above ground. Right now you need to rest. The fire department will be here in a few minutes to get you out safely." He didn't add that they'd instructed him to stay put until they arrived. He was glad he hadn't followed those instructions.

Paige's eyes fluttered open again, looking beyond Jake. "Who is that?" she slurred, lifting her index finger to point to the man on the ground a few feet away. She tried to squint, which resulted in a gasp of pain as her forehead furrowed.

"No one. I'll explain later." Again Jake told her to relax and adjusted the wadded shirt against her open gash.

"Is it bad?" she whispered.

He took a quick peek at the wound. "You're going to need a few stitches," he said. No more than fifteen or twenty, he added silently.

Jake sat on the ground, making sure Paige didn't try to move, and kept a light patter of conversation going. A hard blow to the head was a ready-made recipe for a concussion. He didn't know much about first aid, but he knew it would be best for her to stay awake. He'd seen plenty of rough falls at rodeos. It wasn't smart to sleep them off before being checked by a doctor. Fortunately, he knew that help wasn't far behind him.

CHAPTER THIRTY-FIVE

Voices drifted through the tunnel, a signal the fire department had arrived. Clattering metal echoed within the enclosed space as an extension ladder was lowered from the hotel cellar and braced against a dry, secure support column. Keeping one eye on Paige and the other on the still-unconscious man across from them, Jake waited until the first of the firefighters appeared.

"Couldn't wait for us to get here and lower you down?" Clayton shouted. A bright flashlight beam preceded him. Two additional firefighters followed with a stretcher. Jake didn't bother to answer. The scene itself validated his decision not to wait.

"You're going to need more than one stretcher," Jake said. Without letting go of Paige, he nodded toward the motionless figure on the ground.

"Good work," Clayton called out. He turned to shout orders behind him for a second stretcher before turning back to Jake. "I think it is, anyway. Or...wait. Isn't that Sheriff Myers?"

Jake felt a headache coming on. It was enough of a puzzle to put the pieces together without having to explain them at the same time. "Yes, it's Myers. But you can bet he's not a sheriff. I caught him ready to widen that hole in Paige's forehead."

"You don't say," Clayton said. Confusion clouded his face, but vanished as he got down to business. He looked around, assessed the scene and turned toward the rescue workers.

"Let's get this guy out first," he said, indicating Myers with the beam of his flashlight. Exchanging a knowing look with Jake, he added, "You don't have to go too easy on him. Just get him up there alive. Restrain him until backup from Utica gets down here to sort this mess out."

The firefighters set the stretcher down parallel to Myers, lifted him onto it and headed down the tunnel. Two paramedics arrived with a second stretcher.

"Check her vitals and make sure it's safe to lift her," Clayton said.

The paramedics checked Paige's blood pressure and pulse, and checked for broken bones before moving her. They kept her stretcher level as they raised it and moved slowly toward the hotel cellar.

"Clayton," a firefighter shouted from a distance. "We don't have to go through the hotel's cellar. There's an exit down here."

"You sure about that? There's never been an opening out that way."

"Well, there is now," the voice shouted back. "The wall under the bridge has been dug out with a pick ax. The sheriff's car is parked out there, and that Hollister fella is tied up to that metal grate, poor guy."

Clayton shook his head. Buildings burning down, secret mining tunnels, collapsing cellar floors, the town's homeless man tied up and a visiting reporter unconscious. What was this sleepy town coming to?

Clayton turned to Jake. "Let's get you checked out, too. You're in better shape than the other two, but you could use a few bandages."

Jake brushed himself off and shook his head. "I'm fine. Just a few scrapes and scratches."

"Well, that's what you get when you go tunnel-diving instead of waiting for a ladder," Clayton said.

Jake took the reprimand in stride. The fire chief was right. Using a ladder would have saved him the twelve-foot drop, but he was glad he hadn't waited. He didn't want to contemplate what might have happened if he'd been even a minute later. And he wasn't waiting now, either. He trotted to catch up with Paige's stretcher.

The scene outside the tunnel was chaotic. Myers, now identified as Benny Manetti, was handcuffed to the door of the patrol car he'd confiscated days before. A paramedic attended to Manetti's growing bump on the head, pressing an ice pack against it with surprising enthusiasm. The medic's grin grew wider each time Manetti winced.

As Paige's stretcher emerged from the tunnel, Manetti cursed her out for interfering with his agenda.

"Think you got what you wanted?" he sneered. "It's not like they're gonna let you keep the sapphires, you know. All you had to do was stay out of the way."

"What sapphires?" Paige mumbled. "You mean the paintings?" She tried to lift her head, but was restrained by a paramedic.

"What paintings?" Manetti barked. "Those stupid canvases back there? You weren't looking for sapphires?" His words were cut off by another slap of the ice pack, this one missing his head entirely and landing on his mouth.

"I'm taking this young lady for stitches," the paramedic said.

"I'm coming, too," Jake said.

Hollister, now freed from the metal grate, sat on a barrel off to the side. Mist wrapped cold compresses around his wrists to soothe the burn marks from the ropes that had bound him. His eyes didn't move from the newly dug opening to the tunnel.

A patrol car pulled up, two deputies from Utica emerging. The first deputy opened the back door of his vehicle and helped a third man out. He looked haggard but unharmed.

"Meet the real Sheriff Myers," he said to the crowd. "Found him locked up in a cabin halfway between here and Utica. He's mighty hungry, but otherwise OK."

The second deputy headed for Manetti. He tossed the ice pack on the ground, read him his rights and shoved him in the back of the car.

"We've got free accommodations waiting for you, metal bars and all," he said to Manetti. "Courtesy of the Utica Jail." He turned to Sheriff Myers. "And we'll get you a good meal – or two or three."

"Go on back to the station," the first deputy said. "I'll pull the packages from the tunnel, write up a report and bring back the car Manetti swiped when I'm done."

"I'll help," Clive said. "You can use the gallery."

"Much appreciated," the deputy said. "Right this way." He motioned Clive toward the tunnel.

After a round of handshakes, the group dispersed.

CHAPTER THIRTY-SIX

Mist set a bamboo tray on the center table in the parlor. A pot of green tea sat to one side, surrounded by ceramic mugs, a jar of honey and a bowl of raw sugar. A platter of fresh cinnamon-apple cookies covered the rest of the tray. She filled mugs with tea and offered them to the crowd gathered around the room. Betty took one, as did some of the other townsfolk. Clive, however, excused himself to run back to the gallery. He returned soon after with a bottle of whiskey and half a dozen shot glasses. Whiskey takers soon outnumbered tea drinkers, and Betty retrieved a set of a dozen shot glasses from the hotel dining supply. Even Mist eventually set down her tea and serenely picked up a shot glass.

Paige sat on the couch, a blanket over her lap. Tempting though the whiskey was, she knew better than to indulge. The painkiller she'd been given when the town doctor stitched up her forehead had not yet worn off and was making her woozy enough. Still, her thoughts were clearer than they had been in the early hours of the morning when she'd been pulled out of the tunnel. Once the doc had ruled out a concussion and patched her up, she'd eaten a light meal, soaked in a hot tub and gotten a solid ten hours' sleep. She wasn't yet her usual self, but her curiosity had returned.

Residents of Timberton mingled around the room in animated discussion. Jake sat across the room with Clive, but kept a close watch on Paige. Not more than thirty seconds passed between the affectionate glances he sent her way. Betty and Mist kept busy replenishing cookies and refilling drinks.

Hollister sat not far from the table that held the tea. Though he had tried to return to his usual daytime spot in the town park, Mist had convinced him to come inside the hotel. After the sheriff from Utica had untied him, he seemed more docile than usual and let Mist lead him.

Paige set her mug of tea down on a side table, closed her eyes and let her head fall back against the couch. The conversations around her blended together and soothed her. Timberton's residents had grown to be her friends. As she listened to the murmur of voices, she replayed the events of the morning in her mind, as best she could remember them. She had a vague recollection of Jake leaning over her in the tunnel, followed by the memory of being carried out into the fresh air. Sheriff Myers had been there somewhere...but in handcuffs? No, that didn't make sense. Wasn't he the one who had carried her out? No, wait – that was Jake. Or was it one of the firefighters? And what about the packages inside the tunnel? Hadn't there been packages?

She opened her eyes, looked around the room and sighed. She'd never been much for painkillers. If she'd been more insistent about refusing them when the doctor stitched her forehead up, she'd be having better luck putting everything together.

Jake slid beside Paige and pulled a paper out of his pocket; he unfolded it and smoothed out the creases. He leaned toward Paige and lowered his voice. "I think you'll want to see this."

"From Lambert?" Paige asked, her words sluggish, but her curiosity triggered.

Jake shook his head. "Close, but no. These are from a friend of his at the Smithsonian. Look carefully at the paper, you'll see similarities."

Paige nodded. "This is an infrared image, like the ones Lambert showed us. But it's not the same painting."

"Exactly," Jake said. "They've had this painting at the Smithsonian for some time, hoping to identify the artist. The signature, like the one on Clive's painting and the one from Great Falls, is Silas Wheeler. But, you can see from the underdrawings, this one is by the same, unknown artist who painted Clive's."

Paige took the paper and looked at the markings revealed by the infrared reflectography. "OK, I can see that. But does this really mean anything? There are plenty of artists who do outstanding work. So what if these aren't by Wheeler? It doesn't necessarily make them valuable." Maybe the painkillers were clouding her enthusiasm. She didn't share Jake's excitement. To add to her distraction, a clatter from the middle of the room erupted as an arm reaching for the plate of cookies knocked the bowl of sugar onto the floor. Mist went to the kitchen to fetch a broom.

"Just hear me out," Jake continued. "Lambert's friend at the Smithsonian has had a buyer for that painting for some time. But he held off selling it, hoping to find others for comparison."

"So Clive's painting may be worth more," Paige said.

"Yes, quite a bit more. There's something else, too." Jake grinned.

Paige gave him a puzzled look, waiting for him to explain.

"A lump was found in the painting they've been holding. Turned out it was a small sapphire." Jake waited for the information to sink in.

"A sapphire? You mean…?" Paige's eyes grew wide.

Jake nodded. "Yep, a tiny Yogo, buried in a thick brush stroke of paint. So Lambert sent Clive's painting and the one from Great Falls through another analysis and found sapphires in those pieces, too."

"It sounds like our mystery painter had more than one secret signature." Paige felt her thoughts clicking into focus.

"Exactly," Jake said.

"I could get a second article out of this." A huge smile spread across Paige's face.

"I certainly think so." Jake mirrored her smile. "Maybe you'll even have to extend your stay to write it." His touch on her cheek was hopeful.

"Don't count on it," Paige laughed. "I suspect Susan will know I've gathered enough 'in the field' information to write the rest from the office."

"How about some more tea?" Jake lifted the empty mug beside Paige. He walked to the center table for a refill. Mist had just arrived with the broom and had it aimed at the spilled sugar when Jake suddenly grabbed her arm and stopped her.

"Wait," he said. His tone was sharper than he meant it to be, but he needed to be sure Mist heard him.

Mist simply stopped moving and held the broom by her side. Jake rushed back to Paige, handed the mug back to her and pulled the papers out of her hands. Paige looked into the still-empty mug and then at the empty hand that had just been holding the images of the paintings.

Back at the table, Jake pointed to the sugar on the floor, his voice excited. "Mist, do you see that?" A few other townspeople came over to look. Jake held the papers in front of him, comparing the sugar and the papers. He pointed to a mark that Hollister had just drawn in the sugar.

"Yes," Mist said. "He draws that a lot in the dirt at the park. I've tried to work with him on other letters, but he'll only write this one."

Jake looked again at the papers and back at the floor, a grin spreading across his face. He took a quick picture with his cell phone and then turned back toward Paige.

"Paige, I think you have more of a second story than you think."

CHAPTER THIRTY-SEVEN

"Where's the stash we found in the mining tunnel?" Jake left Hollister retracing the mark in the spilled sugar and turned to Clive.

"It's all at the gem gallery, being inventoried." Clive said. "The deputies needed a place with good lighting to photograph and catalog everything. And they wanted to get the packages out of the tunnel so they could seal it off before anyone else tried to enter. It's not safe in there."

"Probably not," Paige muttered. Still groggy from the painkillers, every statement she made was edged with humor. She twisted sideways and rested her head on the couch.

Jake and Clive exchanged grins.

"Definitely not," Jake added. He smiled at Paige before turning back to Clive.

"What do you say we see how the inventory is going?" Jake thrust a thumb toward the hotel's front door. "I have a feeling I know exactly what's in those packages."

Paige wrinkled her brow as she listened. She'd had a clear look at the packages before her flashlight gave out, as well as at the printed numbers on each one.

"I'm coming with you." Paige leaned forward and made an effort to stand, in spite of disapproval from both Jake and Clive. On the first try, she lost her balance and fell back onto the couch. She ignored another round of pleading for her to rest. Her second attempt at standing was more successful. She held up both hands, refusing help when Jake extended an arm for support.

"You are not leaving me behind. I slept for ten hours, remember?" Paige took a few steps without faltering to prove she was up for a short walk. "The doctor told me to take it easy. He didn't say I had to remain motionless. Besides, I can't just sit around and listen to everyone discussing my 'adventure' as if I'm not even here."

"You're my stubborn girl. I guess there's no sense in trying to change your mind," Jake said.

Paige warmed to the words "my" and "girl."

The scene at the gallery was calm compared to the hotel. Paige took a seat and looked around.

The paintings all had western themes, but the subject matter varied. In some, soft landscapes picked up intricate details of the local area. The essence of the Judith Basin scenery was so real it almost seemed an observer could step into the paintings and become part of the surroundings.

Still others portrayed specific subject matter – bison, horses, wagons and campfires or Native American tribes. Some reflected Russell's style, while others were unique. Paige knew nothing about brush strokes, color tones and other technical details, but she was sure Lambert would have insight to give.

She turned her attention to a deputy taking notes as questions began to form. "There were numbers on the packages," she said.

"Don't worry. I've noted them as I've opened each painting," the deputy commented. "I don't know what they represent, but I've attached the number to the inside frame of each canvas."

"I think I know what the numbers represent," Paige said. "Each one has a meaning."

"Uh oh," Clive said. "She's starting to sound like Mist."

"I'll take that as a compliment," Paige said. "I could use a few lessons from Mist. I think she sees more than those of us who spend our lives rushing around."

Clive was not convinced. "I'll take this as a side effect of those pain killers," he whispered to Jake, who nodded in agreement.

Paige ignored the men's whispers and spoke directly to the deputy. "The numbers are important."

The deputy paused. "If you're asking me what they mean, ma'am, I don't know. I'm just taking inventory."

"Don't worry," Paige said. "Just note which numbers go with which paintings. I have a feeling I can figure out the rest of it."

Jake was beginning to catch on. "You think these are all by the same artist as the one we sent to Lambert?" Jake reached out and traced the initials at the bottom right of one of the paintings. "S. J. W. Silas Wheeler? And that 'J'...."

"I'd like to compare the printing and numbers to..." Paige hesitated. Any mention of the diary in front of the deputy could mean losing her best means of identifying the artist. She rephrased her response. "...to something I read recently."

"No problem," the deputy answered. "I'll give you a list when I'm done. And I'll need you to sign a police report."

Paige nodded and moved back to Clive's desk. Her enthusiasm was running high at the possibilities the paintings might create. But her physical strength was waning. Jake remained with the paintings, walking from one to another. Clive moved outside when his cell phone rang, to keep from disturbing the deputy's work.

Settled in Clive's chair, Paige looked around the gallery. Half of the paintings had been catalogued already and set aside. The deputy was working his way through the second half. Almost all the packages were of similar size save for one that rested on the edge of Clive's desk.

"What's this?" Paige called over to the deputy and indicated the canvas sack.

"You can look in it, if you want. I inventoried the contents before starting in on the paintings," the deputy called to Paige while continuing his note taking. "There's nothing exciting in there. I don't know why we had such a hard time prying it out of that Manetti guy's hands."

I'll be the judge of what's exciting or not, Paige thought as she opened the sack. Hadn't Manetti said something about sapphires as they loaded him into the patrol car? Now, looking into the sack, she could imagine how disappointed he would have been if he'd "escaped" with his precious find. Packed tightly inside the sack were tubes of paint, brushes, a handful of writing implements and a few rags.

Clive re-entered the gallery just as Paige was repacking the bag of artist supplies.

"Well, I'll be darned. That was your other deputy at the jail, wanting to know if I'd ever talked to that Manetti guy before today."

"Had you?" Paige, Jake and the other deputy all asked the question at the same time.

Clive looked bewildered. "No, of course not. But apparently I talked to someone else he knew. A jeweler back east."

"What jeweler?" This time the question came from Jake.

Paige was starting to see a chain of events come together – more specifically, a long chain of misunderstandings. Paige turned to Jake to explain.

"Clive had a few phone calls before I came out here, from jewelers back east who were looking for sapphires. You know, businesses that wanted to build up their inventories before international buyers came in for the conference. Nothing that would have seemed unusual." The whole situation was becoming clearer to Paige as she explained it.

Jake's eyes widened as he listened. He made a point of keeping his voice light as he turned toward Clive. "What did you tell these people when they called?"

"I told them the truth, that I had sapphires I could sell them," Clive said. "It's been a slow year. Heck, I was glad to have a chance to make more sales, especially if stores wanted multiple pieces. And a few did, especially that one guy I told you about." He directed the last comment to Paige.

"You mentioned a guy who talked on and on, seemed a little pushier than the others..." Paige said.

Clive nodded. "Yes, annoying guy, but seemed interested in buying a large amount. Didn't care if they were set or not, just wanted to know how many I could supply."

Jake looked down, kicked a boot heel against the floor and then looked back up. "And what did you tell him?"

"I told him what he wanted to know." Clive said, shrugging his shoulders. "I didn't want to lose a sale, so I said I had a good supply."

The deputy took a call on his radio. Paige and Jake exchanged glances. It only took a moment for Clive to realize what they were all thinking.

"OK, maybe I exaggerated a little," Clive admitted. "That one guy seemed so eager; I played it up a bit. Told him we had our own mines out here and all that. Figured maybe I'd get all his business and he wouldn't call anyone else. But he never called back."

"When was this again?" Paige asked.

Clive scratched his head. "Oh, a few days before you arrived, I think."

"What was the guy's name, Clive? Do you remember?" Paige started to stand up. A pounding stab of pain in her forehead set her back down again.

"I'm sorry, I just don't remember," Clive shrugged.

"Well, I bet I can refresh your memory." The deputy's voice came from the front door, where he was clipping his radio back onto his belt. "That was the station. Manetti spilled the beans. He was hired to come out here, find a big stash of sapphires and deliver the goods to the guy who hired him."

"And who was that?" Paige asked. "Did he say?"

The deputy pulled a notepad out of his pocket and flipped through it. "Looks like the guy's name was Sid." He looked over his notes a second time. "Yes, that's it – Sid, from Manhattan. We've got a call in to the NYPD to pick him up."

Paige closed her eyes and shook her head. "They used me as bait."

"What are you talking about?" Jake's expression was a mix of concern and anger. Clive stood by, trying to follow.

"Sid, the jeweler who told my editor this town was a good home base for an article on sapphire mining," Paige explained. "He must have made calls to find a lucrative supply of sapphires before telling Susan his 'suggestion' of where to send me. Then he and his cohort Manetti used me to lead them here. Figured I'd lead them to Clive's stash of sapphires – which doesn't exist, but they didn't know that."

"Quite a comedy of errors," the deputy quipped as he closed the notebook and headed for the door. "I've left a copy of the report and inventory on the desk back there," he called over his shoulder. "I'll be in touch if we have more questions."

"I'm not sure comedy is the right word for this mess," Jake said. "The town lost a building to fire; Mist lost her livelihood; your homeless resident has been terrorized; and Paige almost lost her life – all for sapphires that never existed to begin with. I don't see much to laugh about in any of that."

Clive collapsed into a chair and dropped his head between his hands. "What have I done?"

"You haven't done anything, Clive," Paige said quickly. "There was no way you could have known that jeweler was fishing for information. I'll be fine; Hollister is fine; and you'll rebuild the café for Mist."

Clive kept his head buried. "But what if...?"

A gust of wind blew the gallery door open as Mist stepped in.

"There have always been 'what ifs' and there always will be." Mist's soothing voice joined the mix as she entered the gallery and walked over to Clive. "We gain nothing by looking at 'what if' instead of simply looking at what is."

Paige felt relief at the sound of Mist's voice. Of all of them, Mist was the most likely to calm Clive down.

"Clive, I'm happy to work with Betty at the hotel. She needs the help. It's good for me to be there right now." Mist placed a hand on Clive's shoulder and bent forward, lowering her voice before adding, "and she's lonely." She waited until his head lifted before she straightened up.

"And as for Hollister," Mist continued, "We are not always who people think we are." She turned and left to go back to the hotel.

"That might be the first thing she's ever said that I've understood," Jake said. "Mist can explain about Hollister, but right now someone here should be resting." He looked at Paige sternly and extended his arm to help her up. Too tired to argue, she stood and leaned against him as they walked back to the hotel.

*   *   *   *

The quilted comforter and shams felt luxurious as Paige eased her aching body down onto the bed. Jake had returned to the gallery to help Clive and Mist check over the list the deputy had left. As curious as Paige was to look at the paintings more closely, her pain and fatigue won. There was only so much a person could manage after a night trapped in a mining tunnel. She owed it to herself to rest.

She forced herself back up one more time to check her cell phone, stepping around remnants of the mess the imposter sheriff had left behind. She hadn't checked her voicemail since the morning, when she'd put in a quick call to the office to tell them she was OK. Susan had been panic-stricken since Jake had called the night before asking if she'd heard from Paige. She'd been so relieved to find out she was safe.

The phone showed she had a new voicemail message. In spite of the comfort of the bed calling to her, she retrieved it.

*Paige, OMG, I just heard what happened. Wild! I'm glad you're OK! So, you probably don't want to hear about work now. Wait, knowing you, you do. No, maybe you don't....*The sound of a hair dryer muffled the next few words...*Anyway, Susan has me on a hunt for Yogos. Not to go with my yoga pants either! Um ... that was a joke. Anyway, I thought I'd ask if you know where I can find some, since you're out there where they grow them* ...at this point there was a delay while Brandi sputtered into laughter before continuing...*You know what I mean, Paige. It's not like I THINK they grow on trees. Anyway, we're still having trouble getting some of the jewelers to run ads unless they can get Yogos in stock before the convention. Let me know if you have any idea where I can find them. What's even WORSE is the one totally gargantuan ad I had lined up fell through. Sid's Jewelers, can you believe it? After he told us where you should go in the first place?...*the hair dryer resumed, cutting off a section of the next statement... *boarded up, can you EVEN believe it? GONE, just like that. Too totally bizarro, I'm telling you. Anyway, see if you can check around for me. I'm running out of time to pin the ads down and I'm getting my hair beaded tomorrow, so that cuts into my day, too. So, ciao! Oh, and feel better. Ciao! Wait, I already said that. Bye!*

Paige smiled as she fell off to sleep. Two dilemmas, one solution. Clive had enough inventory to supply a few New York jewelers, which could prompt them into purchasing ads. And the sales would help get him started rebuilding the café.

CHAPTER THIRTY-EIGHT

Betty smoothed the front of her apron, a bright, cotton print of intertwined roses and daisies. Catching a glimpse of herself in the mirror next to the sink, she could see the subtle glow in her reflection. How long had it been since she'd bothered with makeup? A long time. But Mist had encouraged her to add a touch of rouge to her cheeks that morning, and she was glad she had. She felt younger and more alive than she'd felt in a long time.

Betty circled the crowded kitchen table, reaching between shoulders to refill mugs with freshly brewed coffee. She'd tried to shoo the enthusiastic crowd into the parlor where there was more room, but the animated participants in the conversation weren't about to leave the cozy kitchen.

Paige sat on a bar stool at one end of the counter, a fresh bandage on her forehead and an expression far more alert than the one she'd worn the day before. Clive sat beside her, his hands wrapped around the steaming beverage. He did a quick double take after Betty filled his mug.

Across from them, Jake leaned forward, the smooth, tan skin of his hands and wrists blending in with the wooden countertop. Oblivious to chatter around him, he was focused on several papers and photographs.

Mist stood a few feet away, serene in a flowing, embroidered dress in aqua tones. Her hair fell loosely around her shoulders, one side held back behind her ear with a branch of dried lavender. To her immediate right sat the most unlikely of the morning visitors to the hotel kitchen. Having been gently coaxed inside by Mist for the second day in a row, Hollister kept his eyes fixed on an untouched mug of coffee.

"Explain it again, Jake," Clive said. "Who is this Smithsonian guy?"

"He's a friend of Professor Lambert, the art appraiser we consulted in Cody," Jake explained. "Lambert called him to get another opinion on the underdrawings that were found when your painting was analyzed."

Jake swiveled a photograph around to face Clive, pointing to the markings the infrared light had revealed. Clive shook his head. "I saw these before, but they still just look like scribbles to me."

"Well, in a way, that's all they are," Jake agreed. "But this is where it gets interesting." He turned a second photograph toward Clive and then a third. "In this second photo you see a similar 'squiggle,' as you call it. This photograph is from a painting that the Smithsonian expert has. He's been trying to identify the artist who painted it for years. He has a buyer for it."

"Well, that's great," Clive said. "But what does that have to do with me?"

"Look at the two photos closely. You see how the markings are identical? These were painted by the same artist and both disguised as Silas Wheeling's work." Jake waited while Clive compared the two images. "That means the buyer who wants to buy the painting at the Smithsonian also wants to buy yours."

"Great," Clive said. "Sell it. Get a few hundred for it, and we'll put it toward rebuilding the café."

Jake smiled. "I think you're looking at more than a few hundred, Clive. According to the Smithsonian expert, these paintings are worth about five thousand each, at least."

Clive looked dumbfounded. "They're just paintings! My truck isn't even worth that much."

"That's the truth," Betty quipped. Her comment received a round of laughter and a well-earned smirk from Clive.

"It has to do with the technique," Mist pointed out. "The lightness of the brush strokes, the complementary use of colors, the general feeling the pieces achieve – those all make a difference in the value. At first glance, many paintings look similar. But if you step closer, the details are different. And if you step away, the overall effect is unique."

"Well, sell it, then!" Clive lifted his coffee mug in the air as if to make a toast, then brought it to his mouth and emptied it in one gulp. "Let's get this little lady's new café started first thing in the spring." He stood up, pushed the empty mug away and smiled at Mist.

"Not so fast, Clive," Jake said, grinning. "There's a little more to the story." He winked at Paige, who responded with a knowing smile.

"Now what?" Clive asked, sitting back down. "I should have known it wasn't that easy." Betty poured him another mug full of coffee.

This time Paige took over.

"We took a closer look at the paintings we found in the tunnel. We'll need to send them out for analysis to be sure, but we think they'll come back with identical underdrawings. And a tiny sapphire hidden in each one, too." She waited for the information to sink in. It only took a few seconds before Clive's eyes grew wide.

"You think all those paintings are by the same artist?" Clive looked from face to face. Clearly, they all thought so.

"Well, I'll be a doggone muskrat's grandpa!" Clive's mouth dropped open, but closed just as quickly. "Wait a minute," he said. "I suppose the one I had in the gallery is mine, since I found it in the basement of my own building. But those other paintings were hidden away underground. Who do they belong to? Or do they belong to anyone?"

"I think I know the answer to that," Paige said. She left the kitchen, returning a few moments later with the partial diary. "I found this one of the first nights I was here. I believe it belonged to Silas Wheeler. The initials in the front are SW and the angry entries fit the personality you described to me, Clive."

Clive stood up and moved over by Paige, where he could see the diary. "SW...Yes, that is the way he signed his early paintings. But the ones I've seen have usually been signed SJW, especially those he had me selling to tourists."

"That's because he was passing off someone else's work," Paige filled in. "In the diary entries I found, Silas was enraged that his teacher, Charles Russell, never acknowledged his ability as an artist. Of course, we know from his paintings – the early ones, which were actually his – that he was a mediocre artist. He was thrilled to discover a student he could exploit."

"So you're saying he passed off his student's paintings as his own by adding his initials to the signature?" Betty looked appalled.

"That's exactly what he did," Paige said. "That's why the underdrawings show the curved mark under the letter 'J.' The real artist traced his initial before painting over it. Look at the photo from the infrared analysis of the piece from your gallery."

Jake pushed the photo from Lambert's analysis out to the middle of the table for everyone to see. It clearly showed the sketched "J" under the "SJW."

"My, oh my, that is a crying shame, I dare say," Betty exclaimed. "Taking advantage of someone's talent like that." She stood next to Clive, looking at the photo and shaking her head. "How did he manage to do that, anyway – steal all those paintings without the student knowing? That doesn't make sense."

"What makes sense to one person doesn't always make sense to another. Reality and perception are not always the same," Mist said.

"Here we go," Clive whispered to no one in particular. Betty hushed him.

Mist looked at Jake, who nodded. Anticipating Paige's confusion, Jake winked at her again. Paige sat back, knowing she'd missed a few pieces of the puzzle while dazed the previous day.

Picking up the picture of the underdrawing, as well as the one Jake hadn't shown yet, Mist set them in front of Hollister, side by side. She stepped back and watched his gaze fall on the photos.

Minutes passed with no response from the old man. Jake checked his watch. Paige drummed her fingers against the leg of her jeans. Clive cleared his throat; Betty elbowed him. Mist just waited.

Hollister's face remained expressionless as he stared at the two photos. At one point he dropped his head and simply looked at the floor. Jake reached out to retrieve the pictures, but Mist motioned for him to wait. Another thirty seconds went by before Hollister raised his head again, but when he did his eyes held a glimmer that hadn't been there before. Paige and the others were silent as they watched the old man raise a shaky arm toward the first photo and trace his finger along the letter "J." And no one took so much as a shallow breath as he moved his arm to trace the same curved outline in the photo of the spilled sugar from the day before.

Betty was the first to gasp. "No, it's not possible!" Her reaction was reflected in the faces of the others.

"But the paint dated back sixty years or so when Lambert analyzed it," Paige said, turning first toward Jake and then toward the others. "That would mean..." She paused, mid-sentence, recalling the passages in the diary, after which she took a good look at Hollister's aged, wrinkled hands and face. "Yes, that would be about right."

"Time is meaningless when searching for a part of your soul," Mist offered as explanation. It all seemed to make sense to her. "We never stop looking when a part of us is lost."

Mist turned to face the old man, extending one arm toward him. She paused just inches away from his hand and waited for approval before touching him. Sensing permission in his eyes, she wrapped her hand around his gnarled fingers, covered it with her other hand and spoke.

"Your name is Jonas," Mist said, her words smooth and calm. "I don't know if you understand, but I do. We do." Mist looked around the room, making sure to include the others in the conversation before returning to face the old man. "You have been searching for a part of you that was missing for a very long time. And now you have found it."

"All this time we've watched him and never knew he was trying to find anything," Clive said. "Did he even know what he was looking for?"

"It's not necessary to know what you're searching for in order to know you are searching. Or to find it," Mist answered, releasing Hollister's hands. "Haven't you ever found something by chance, only to realize later you were looking for it all along?"

Jake looked at Paige and smiled – a smile that was promptly returned. Betty blushed to match the color of her rouge and ran her hands across the front of her apron. Clive cleared his throat again and looked into his coffee mug. Hollister traced the letter "J" in one of the photos again.

"I thought so," Mist said, surveying the group. Extending her arms to the front, she rested her fingertips against the edge of the table. In her own unique way, she rested her case.

"But, I still don't understand," Betty murmured. She was too polite to demand more information in front of Hollister, but too curious not to want more explanation.

Mist moved closer to Hollister and gently placed a hand on his shoulder as if to allow him to feel included in the discussion. She faced the rest of the group.

"I am neither a doctor of the physical body nor a specialist in matters of mind and spirit," Mist said. "All I can offer is my best guess, based upon my experience during this lifetime."

Clive felt a preventative nudge from Betty before he could react to Mist's implication that a person's earthly journey might not be limited to a single lifetime.

"There was a student in one of my art classes in Santa Cruz," Mist continued, "who had an amazing aptitude for drawing. All you had to do was put a pen in his hand, and the most elaborate sketches would emerge – entire cities, detailed right down to street numbers, for example. Or a night sky filled with constellations – not two or three, but forty or fifty – all drawn perfectly to scale. Yet, once he set the pen down, he retreated into a shell. His motor skills were impaired, and he didn't make eye contact with other students. Our professor explained the unusual contradictions in his behavior as a case of 'Savant Syndrome.'"

"You mean like in that Dustin Hoffman movie?" Clive asked.

"Yes, like in *Rainman,*" Mist answered.

Clive scratched his head. "But that was about math, wasn't it? These are paintings."

Mist nodded. "In that particular movie, yes, the character's exceptional skill was math. But the syndrome itself can manifest in other areas like art or music."

Paige watched Hollister as Mist explained. His hand was tracing the photograph again, his eyes never wavering as the voices around him rose and fell.

"In one of the diary entries," Mist said, "Silas noted that it was easy to remove each painting when it was finished and replace it with a blank canvas. As you can see, when Hollister is drawing – or sketching, tracing, searching for pebbles or painting – he's quite narrowly focused. He is oblivious to anything around him. Unfortunately, that explains why Silas was able to steal and hide his paintings."

Mist left the room and returned with the diary pages she'd found in the laundry room wall. The story came together as each person took turns reading Silas's entries aloud. Mist started and then passed the diary to Paige. Clive read the last three entries aloud, and everyone in the room imagined his voice was Silas's. Hollister was the only person in the room who wasn't riveted.

May 18, 1955

I cannot tell if Jonas hears me when I speak. What a delight it is to have a student who doesn't chatter senselessly or talk back with the arrogance that goes with a preposterous ego. Oh how I tire of the self-absorption of many artists. Still, it makes it difficult to know what he does understand, though I assume most everything passes him by.

August 2, 1955

J. doesn't try to hold onto the paintings when he finishes them. I'm careful to place a new canvas on his easel as I'm removing a finished work. This way, his eyes are immediately focused on the blank surface. Even though I can't get inside his mind – not that I care what goes on in there, as long as what comes out is lucrative – he does have an expression of concentration when he looks at an empty canvas. Sometimes it can take hours for him to start. One time he sat an entire day, staring at the empty canvas on his easel, and never picked up a brush. He simply arrived, sat down, stared straight ahead for hours, stood up and left. Of course, those are lost days and they frustrate me.

Nov. 17, 1955

Tally: Landscapes (212 – 213) – 2, Tribal Conflicts (233 – 234) – 2, Covered Wagons (244 – 246)– 3, Horses – (261 – 262) - 2, Bison (286) – 1, Dust Storm (292) – 1, Wolves (257 – 258) – 2

March 22, 1956

Sold a Dust Storm painting (292) and have a possible sale for one of the horse pieces.

July 10, 1956

I found J. in the studio today, absorbed in a new painting. Marvelous! It is a campfire scene, with two rustic wagons in the background and half a dozen men in the foreground, busy with tasks. To one side, a wolf hovers, undetected, his neck low to the *ground, his eyes aglow from the fire's reflection. A coffee pot has tipped over, the lid tumbling. A scarf angles out from the edge of a stick in the ground. I could almost feel the wind, looking at it. Such detail – this one will undoubtedly fetch a good price.*

October 22, 1956

It is astounding, what this young man creates. And with such ease! The smooth transition between what his mind sees and what evolves on paper is quite remarkable. The results of his work should please me, but they don't. I feel only fury. Yet it is lucrative fury, so I continue to tolerate the insult that his talent stabs at me.

May 5, 1957

What a lucky break, having J. stumble into my life. The man's too dense to keep track of his own shadow. Stupid fool. He forgets each painting as soon as it's out of his sight, a perfect set-up for me. I can already see the dollar signs. Today, as I stored away one of his finished pieces, I could not resist throwing my head back and roaring with laughter, just at the thought of what the future holds for me.

August 22, 1957

Great news! The painting I sent out to Cody a few weeks ago has sold, bringing not only a pretty fee, but words of praise for its vibrant colors and sense of action. It is high time I received the validation I deserve. I'm quite proud of myself. I've sent several additional pieces. I feel confident they will do as well, if not better.

April 23, 1958

A disturbing thing happened today. J. seemed distracted, not fixated on his work, as he usually is. His eyes roamed the room, but focused on nothing in particular. I could tell he was searching. His gaze swept the ceiling, the floor, the tabletops, the windowsill, just about everywhere, though it never lingered. At one point he stood up, set his paintbrush down and crossed the room, stopping in front of a stack of shelves. He picked up an old, chipped coffee mug and looked inside it. He then did the same with another, and another. Eventually he returned to his painting and sat down calmly, as if he had never left the easel at all. It's the first I've seen of this behavior from him. It is probably nothing, yet it worries me.

July 7, 1958

I allowed J. to keep a painting today – a rather tame one, at that, nothing more than a landscape. It was a calculated move, designed to keep him from being curious about the storage of the others. I tell him he must not linger once a piece is finished. Out of sight, it frees the mind to dive into the next one. The completed works will stay completed, but the new ones will not come to exist if focus isn't maintained. I am doing him a favor by removing them. He believes me, silly boy. And why not? I almost believe myself.

August 5, 1958

J. did not show up this morning. I waited for hours, but finally grew impatient and decided to go out searching. I found him not far away, sitting in the empty lot in the center of town. He didn't seem surprised to see me. Sometimes I wonder if he even recognizes me. I waved for him to follow, but he didn't respond. I tried again several times before losing my temper and giving him a tongue-lashing – in vain, of course. Eventually, I turned back and headed for the studio. Shortly after, he followed.

October 14, 1958

    J. continues to wander. I have half a mind to give him the paintings, as I grow weary with fatigue. But what of my legacy? If I show the pieces that are hidden, discredit will come to those already revealed. I cannot take the money from the newer works with me to the grave, but I can leave my legacy behind. I deserve as much.

February 10, 1959

    I no longer feel safe keeping J's paintings in the cellar. He has taken to wandering more, which is, in itself, annoying. The less he focuses, the less he produces. But, more worrisome is the fear he will find the stash. I half suspect he wouldn't even know what he found, but I can't take that chance. There's no way to know what goes on in that confused mind of his — what he might recognize and what he wouldn't. How does a man go through life with a brain that simple? Yet have the talent he has?

March 9, 1959

    Tally: Landscapes (212 – 216) – 5, Tribal Conflicts (233 – 236) – 4, Covered Wagons (244 – 246)– 3, Horses – (261 – 263) - 3, Bison (286 – 287) – 2, Dust Storm (293) – 1, Wolves (257 – 258) – 2, Winter Scenes (226 – 227) – 2

CHAPTER THIRTY-NINE

Jake set the bulky canvas against the gallery wall and turned back to face Paige. "How many more do we have left?" He watched as she tallied lines down the length of a legal size paper.

"Fourteen," Paige answered. "Three landscapes, four covered wagon scenes, one campfire, two bison groupings, one wolf pack and three tribal gatherings." She paused, checking the list again. "Yes, that's right, fourteen pieces. Not counting the sack of painting supplies, which we need to send, as well. Lambert said the lab wants to test the age of the paint, though I'm sure it'll match that on the paintings."

"Why would Silas have packed away the paints?" Jake stepped back from the paintings that awaited shipping and tossed the question over his shoulder. Paige watched his self-confident stance from the rear. There was something about the way he shifted his weight onto one hip and folded his arms across his chest that made his clothing fall snugly across the muscular contours of his body. She forgot for a moment that he had asked a question at all.

"Paige?" Jake repeated, uncrossing his arms and thrusting his thumbs into the front pockets of his jeans. Paige sighed. That was no better. Would she ever be able to concentrate around this man?

"I know you're focused on the inventory, but did you hear me? Why do you think Silas hid the paints?"

"I think he wanted paint that would match identically if he needed to touch up any of the paintings. He planned to come back for them, but never did. Clive said he drank himself to death."

Paige handed Jake a painting depicting a lone Blackfoot overlooking a lush valley. The scene felt rich with possibilities. Paige ran her finger down the inventory sheet and marked off the corresponding number.

"So the paintings stored in the tunnel were all by Hollister...er...Jonas and hidden by Silas way back when?" Jake said.

Paige nodded. "That's the way it looks. The later diary pages Mist found indicate Silas accessed the hiding place from the cellar of the café building. That matches the location of the paintings I found. We'll know for sure when Lambert gets the infrared results back on each piece."

"Well, it looks like Clive won't have any problem rebuilding the café if these fetch the kind of price that Smithsonian guy was talking about," Jake said. He reached to take the next painting from Paige – a disarray of pots and pans falling off the back end of a lop-sided covered wagon.

"Jake," Paige exclaimed. "Clive won't keep the money from these. He and Mist already discussed this; Clive took the practical approach, and Mist, of course, the philosophical." Paige set the paperwork down and sighed. She stood up, stretched and relayed the discussion as best she could.

"They both agree that the paintings belong to the true artist. After they're authenticated, Clive will keep any that Silas actually painted, since he's no longer living. But the ones that Hollister painted will be sold, the proceeds put into a trust for Hollister's care. He keeps returning to the area under the trestle to sleep at night, but Mist is working with him. She thinks she'll be able to coax him into sleeping inside one of the hotel rooms before long. He already comes up there for meals."

"Of course he does. Everyone goes there now that Mist is cooking." Jake laughed, but then grew serious. "Unfortunately, that still leaves Clive in a bind for rebuilding the café, doesn't it?"

"Yes and no," Paige answered. "He may not get anything from the paintings. But he has an opportunity to sell his Yogo jewelry. Brandi's been having trouble getting jewelers to commit to the ads for the sapphire article. They want Yogos on hand for impulse buys by conference attendees. If they can't get the sapphires in stock, they don't want to put money into advertising. Clive has some nice pieces. Not enough to supply everyone who's asking for them, but enough to sell to a few stores."

"What happened to the guy who hired Manetti?" Jake reached over as Paige handed him a landscape of the hills directly behind Timberton. Holding it at arm's length, he recognized the sketched outline of the older town buildings.

"Sid? He's long gone," Paige said. "Shop cleaned out in the middle of the night. Disappeared without a trace. Must've known Manetti would sing. Susan feels terrible about falling for Sid's story. But how was she to know?"

Jake whistled. "Isn't that something."

"Isn't what something?" Clive's booming voice came from the back office, quickly followed by the sound of a door slamming.

"I didn't know you were here, Clive," Paige said. She marked off another item on the paperwork and glanced up as Clive responded.

"I wasn't. Just came in the back door. I had me a little business to attend to over at the hotel." Clive said, as he emerged from his office. Paige noted a subtle change in his appearance. He looked taller, bolder and more confident than she'd seen him before. And he was smiling.

"Dinner's at six tonight," Clive announced. "Mist is cooking up something special. Everyone's invited."

"I think anything Mist cooks up is special," Jake said.

"Well, that's the truth, ain't it?" Clive laughed. "But I'm just telling you what she said – six o'clock. Better be there or you might be left with no other choice but fast food. Wild Bill's not cooking any more, goes to the hotel every night. I think he's got a thing for Mist's maple-glazed sweet potatoes. Then again, it's not like he had customers, anyway."

"Clive," Paige said, ignoring his tangent, "You can't get fast food around here."

"Why, sure you can," Clive said. "You just take a left up there by the park."

"Really?" Paige and Jake spoke simultaneously.

"Yes, really," Clive said. "After that left, just head on down the highway about twenty-two miles and take another left when you come to a big ol' cluster of propane tanks, just after you pass over the third cattle guard. Then, about eight miles past that, there's a red barn – paint's kinda faded, but if it ain't dark yet, you'll see it. You take a hairpin turn just past that, go another five miles or so and it'll be on the right side. Best corndogs you'll ever have."

Paige and Jake exchanged glances.

"Six o'clock sounds fine, Clive. Thanks," Paige said.

Clive looked at the progress of the pre-shipping preparation. "How's it going, anyway? When are those art people coming to pick all this up?"

Paige couldn't help smiling. "Clive, those 'art people,' as you call them, are historians from the Smithsonian Institute, and, to answer your question, looks like we have eleven packages to go."

"Make that twelve." A voice from the gallery's front doorway interrupted the conversation. One of the deputies from Utica stood in the store with a dusty flour sack. Cradled in the deputy's hands, it looked like a small, dirty off-white football. Paige half expected the deputy to run back and throw long.

"Of course, the sack," Paige said, glancing up briefly and returning to her paperwork. "That makes twelve. Though I thought…." Her voice trailed off as she turned toward a table against the far gallery wall. The rumpled sack of painting supplies was sitting where it had been placed earlier. She turned back to the deputy, perplexed.

"I don't understand. We have the sack right here."

The deputy nodded. "Yes, ma'am. Everything from the tunnel is here. Except for the sack I'm holding, that is. We missed it when we unloaded the trunk of the patrol car. Apparently one of the picture frames pushed it into a back corner. It fell into a slot behind the spare tire. We found it late last night."

Paige sighed and started toward the deputy. More paint to add to the inventory list. Silas had certainly played it safe, stashing away two batches of supplies. How much touching up had he thought he'd have to do? Paige reached for the sack, only to have the deputy hold up one hand to stop her.

"I think Clive might want to open this one," the deputy said.

Paige wondered if she imagined the faint smile on the officer's face. She turned to Clive, shrugged her shoulders and motioned him over. Clive raised his eyebrows and casually grabbed the sack. He headed to the worktable, setting it down under the bright lights. As the others gathered around, he emptied the contents.

In all the years Paige had visited the Atlantic shoreline on bright, sunny days, she'd never seen a sea of sparkling blue that matched the one that splashed across the worktable when Clive emptied the sack. Like cornflower blue stardust, the sapphires tumbled against the golden grain of the wood surface, flashing as brightly as fireworks. Paige had to blink just to focus.

Clive dropped the empty sack in shock, leaned against the edge of the table and tried to breathe. Jake let out a long, low whistle. Paige continued to blink, unable to pull her thoughts together. And the deputy stood by, waiting for someone to speak.

"Are these...?" Clive's voice cracked and squeaked like an adolescent boy's. He paused before trying again. "Are these...?" Again, he stopped. It was too much to put into words.

"You're Clive Barnes, is that correct?" The deputy leaned forward and tried to look at Clive straight on, attempting to get the shaky gallery owner's full attention. Clive lifted glazed eyes from the sparkling gems and simply nodded.

"Well, all right then," the deputy said, "these are yours, Clive."

"Is there any way this could be a mistake?" Paige finally managed to speak.

"No, ma'am," the deputy said. "When I found these last night, I went back through every old theft report I could find, decades of them." He faced Clive.

"Clive, when you filed your report way back, you turned in a detailed copy of your inventory – every single stone, each style, cut and size. These match that report exactly. Some of the smallest stones are missing, but the rest are all here." He pulled a folded paper out of his pocket and handed it to Clive. "There's no way anyone else is the rightful owner."

With a tip of his deputy's hat, he left, pausing only to advise Clive to put the sapphires in the gallery safe.

Clive sat down in the closest chair. He looked back and forth between Paige and Jake, shaking his head in disbelief.

"So these were squirreled away with all those paintings – all these years?" Clive asked. "We've been walking right on top of them?"

"Seems to be the case," Paige said. "Looks like Silas stole more than just Hollister's paintings."

"Must be why he left town when he did," Clive mused. "Figured he'd bury the sapphires along with everything else and come back for it all later. He just never made it."

"Clive, if you've gotten your wind back, you need to pack those up and put them in the safe," Paige said. "Jake and I'll finish checking the last of the paintings while you do that. Then we can all go over to the hotel."

Clive nodded and stood up. "It won't take long to lock these up. And I do believe my nerves have drained enough energy to build up an appetite.

"Oh, one more thing, you two," Clive said. "If you could hold off saying anything to Betty or Mist about this right away, I'd appreciate it. I've got a few things to arrange."

CHAPTER FORTY

The blended aromas of garlic, butter and rosemary greeted
Paige as she stepped into the lobby of the hotel. She closed
her eyes and took a deep breath. What else was mixed in
there? A touch of fennel? Lemon, maybe? Shallots? Whatever
it was, her mouth was watering before she even closed the
front door.

"Is that you, Paige?" Betty's voice came from the
direction of the parlor, where Paige found the hotelkeeper
arranging contrasting heights of snipped spruce branches in
canning jars. The room's velvet couch and overstuffed
armchairs had been pushed against the walls. A half dozen
card tables filled the center space, surrounded by folding
chairs and covered with mismatched tablecloths. A few early
birds had already claimed their places. Mist had seated
Hollister at a corner table.

"No one's dining on the front steps tonight, I take it,"
Paige said. Seating had been haphazard since the café burned
down, but townsfolk had always managed to find a spot to sit
and balance a plate.

"Mist's orders," Betty said. "It's been fine having people
come through the kitchen and grab a meal the last few nights.
But if the hand that feeds you tells you to sit down, I figure
you'd better sit or go hungry."

"Sounds like a wise decision," Paige said. "Let me help you with those," she added, taking two of the evergreen arrangements. Once the quaint jars were in place, she made a beeline for the kitchen to see if Mist needed help.

Mist shooed all new arrivals to the kitchen out to the parlor. The improved seating arrangements were popular with the townsfolk, who found their spots around the room. Wild Bill took a place next to Ernie. The candy storeowner joined Sadie, who had nabbed a table near the front window. Clayton and his crew of firefighters fell into chairs on the far side of the room. They leaned forward to exchange viewpoints on a brush fire they had extinguished that afternoon, but sat back abruptly when the fragile, folding table shifted under their weight.

Jake entered and threw a jacket over the back of a chair, claiming three other seats as reserved for Paige, Betty and Clive. He knew better than to reserve one for Mist, who would insist on gliding around to attend to everyone's needs.

"Clive will be here after he finishes up at the gallery," Jake announced.

"Men," Betty huffed under her breath. "There's always something." In spite of her reproachful tone, Jake caught her sneaking a look at the parlor mirror to check her appearance.

Paige emerged from the kitchen with baskets of dinner rolls balanced in her arms. As she set one on each table, the warm scent of freshly baked bread filled the room.

By the time Clive showed up, salads had been pushed aside, replaced with generous servings of roast chicken and garlic mashed potatoes. He sat next to Betty, picked up a knife and fork and emptied the dinner plate in record time. He followed that with seconds and then stood up.

"I have a speech to make," he said, tapping a spoon against his water glass. "I've run into a bit of good luck. Now,

I'm not going into any details, but something I lost many years ago has been found. It's gonna give me a little windfall to help with some things around Timberton."

Cheers went up around the room. Paige caught a twinkle in Mist's eye as she passed by the table. Was something up? Or was Mist simply entertained by Clive's sly understatement? "A little windfall" hardly came close to describing what Clive had recovered that day.

"Now, hold on, everyone." Clive tapped his spoon against the glass again to settle the crowd. "Let me explain. First of all, we'll need to wait until next spring, but we'll get Moonglow rebuilt." He waited for a round of applause to subside.

"In the meantime, I think we oughta fix up the hotel here and get a temporary restaurant going for the winter. And, personally, I say we start with some sturdy tables and chairs," he said. More cheers erupted, this time from the firefighters' table.

"Why would you want to build the café here and then have to do it all over again in the spring?" Betty said. "That's not too practical, Clive."

"Well, for one thing, we have to eat somewhere. It might as well be here," Clive said. "I can't think of anywhere else we'd want to go." A few people turned to grin at Bill Guthrie.

"And for another thing, Betty, I've got something to ask you," Clive said. He shifted his weight back and forth, looking like a nervous schoolboy called to the front of the class. Paige watched, half expecting him to run for the door, but he stood his ground.

Betty braced her hands against the table. "Now, don't go scaring me like that, Clive. I've got my hands full enough around here without you causing trouble."

A voice from the firefighters' table carried across the room. "I'm not sure what kind of trouble that is, Betty, having him fixing things all the time."

"What're you talking about, Clayton?" Betty said. "You've been helping out around here for as long as I can remember."

"No, ma'am," Clayton said. "Just keepin' your fire extinguisher up to date and pullin' Sadie's cat out of that tree behind the hotel now and then. You know it runs away from the Curl 'N Cue every time a hair dryer turns on."

"And you, Ernie," Betty said, pointing to a different table. "Haven't you done a few things around here?"

Ernie shook his head. "Sorry, Betty, Pop's Parlor takes up all of my time."

Betty eyes grew wide as she turned to Clive and searched his face. "Why, Clive, you've been the one fixing things, all this time? Why would you do that?"

"Don't you know why, Betty, after all these years?"

The light chatter around the room fell to a hush as it became clear the usual banter between Clive and Betty had changed.

"Because you're my girl, Betty," Clive said. "You always have been. I just never had the nerve to ask you to be."

"I might have said yes way back then, you silly old fool – or maybe not."

"Then I'm going to ask you now." Clive stood tall and looked into Betty's eyes. "Betty, will you be my girl?"

Betty paused, whether to think over her answer or to make Clive endure a few stressful seconds, no one knew.

"Well now, Clive, I think I'd like that."

Betty jumped as Clive let out a wild hoot, took her face in both hands and planted a kiss smack on her lips. A burst of laughter filled the parlor, followed by high fives, glasses clinking and a few enthusiastic whistles.

Releasing Betty, Clive pulled a gold broach from his pocket and pinned it on the scalloped collar of her dress. Paige recognized the design from Clive's display case. The Yogo sapphires above the sculpted hotel sparkled under the parlor lights.

"Does that mean I can make a list of everything that needs fixing?" Betty's attempt to be serious didn't hide her smile.

"I'd say that's a fair request," Clive said.

Mist emerged from the kitchen with plates of hot apple-cherry cobbler. Betty took a seat and motioned for others to sit down.

"Sometimes timing in life is perfect," Mist whispered, as she set a dish of the freshly baked dessert in front of Paige.

"And other times it isn't," Paige added softly. Once again, she felt torn, just as she had the last time she'd left to go back to New York.

"That doesn't mean it won't ever be."

Lost in thought, Paige first believed Clive spoke the words. It only took a moment to realize she was wrong. As she felt Jake's strong hand cover hers, she turned to face him.

"No," she said, a smile spreading across her face. "It doesn't mean it won't ever be."

ACKNOWLEDGEMENTS

Heartfelt thanks go to the many people who helped bring The Moonglow Café to life.

My amazing editor, Elizabeth Christy, is responsible not only for making this manuscript shine, but for keeping me sane during the process, as well as keeping Paige from bumping her head too many times.

I owe thanks to beta readers Carol Anderson and Jay Garner for their excellent plot suggestions and to Carol for her proofreading abilities. Tim at Book Design and More deserves thanks for his patience while teaching me a few tricks of the trade. And Keri Knutson at Alchemy Book Covers deserves a standing ovation for cover design, as well as several bonus rounds of insightful advice.

Though the town of Timberton is fictional, some of the initial ideas for the book stemmed from a visit to Philipsburg, MT, many years ago. The Broadway Hotel, the Sapphire Gallery and the Granite County Museum all contributed background knowledge for the story.

As always, I am grateful to family members and friends for believing in me. Without their support and encouragement, The Moonglow Café would still be an unpolished sapphire, waiting to be discovered.